What reviewers said about
DAEMON HALL

"Readers will get chills imagining the terrors that can exist after dark. Nance crafts a compelling novel by giving insight into each character's fears as well as bringing the reader a dose of death, demons, and the paranormal."—*Voya*

"Nance offers a smoothly written, clever framework for relaying ten scary stories, and horror fans will appreciate classic elements like the spooky house that seems to be alive, the evocation of Agatha Christie's *And Then There Were None*, and the one guest who must be left behind. . . . These tales are enjoyably creepy and straight-up fright-night fun."
—*The Bulletin of the Center for Children's Books*

"Readers looking for creepy chills and thrills will find plenty of satisfaction in this fast-paced book."—*Booklist*

"The stories in this gripping page-turner, as well as the drama of the frightened teens dropping out one by one, will keep readers on the edge of their seats."—*School Library Journal*

RETURN TO
DAEMON HALL
Evil Roots

Andrew Nance

with illustrations by Coleman Polhemus

Christy Ottaviano Books

Henry Holt and Company ✦ New York

Henry Holt and Company, LLC
Publishers since 1866
175 Fifth Avenue
New York, New York 10010
macteenbooks.com

The poem on p. 49 reprinted by permission from
Arnold Lobel, *Whiskers and Rhymes,* © 1985,
Harper Collins Publishers.

Library of Congress Cataloging-in-Publication Data
Nance, Andrew.
Return to Daemon Hall : evil roots / Andrew Nance ;
with illustrations by Coleman Polhemus. — 1st ed.
p.   cm.
"Christy Ottaviano books."
Summary: Wade and Demarius go to author Ian Tremblin's home as judges
of the second writing contest but soon are mysteriously transported to Daemon Hall, where
they and the three finalists must tell—and act out—the stories each has written.
ISBN 978-0-8050-8748-2 (hc)
[1. Authors—Fiction.   2. Authorship—Fiction.   3. Haunted houses—Fiction.
4. Storytelling—Fiction.   5. Contests—Fiction.   6. Horror stories.]
I. Polhemus, Coleman, ill.   II. Title.   III. Title: Evil roots.
PZ7.N143Ret 2011   [Fic]—dc22   2010048609

First edition—2011 / Designed by Véronique Lefèvre Sweet

Printed in the United States of America

1 3 5 7 9 10 8 6 4 2

Unique words have untold power.
I once uttered *smitten* and claimed my life partner.
JoAnn, I'm still smitten.

RETURN TO
DAEMON HALL
Evil Roots

Horror Author Ian Tremblin Stuns Publishing World

From Staff

In a classic here-we-go-again moment, horror author Ian Tremblin has announced another writing contest geared toward his teen readers. It was less than a year ago that his first contest resulted in the death of one contestant and the commitment of another to a mental institution. When negligent homicide charges were dropped and several lawsuits were settled out of court, it was thought that Tremblin would maintain a low profile.

"Like a criminal in hiding? Look, the death of Chelsea Flynt was heartbreaking," the author said in response to this story. "And everyone is asking, 'Why another contest after such tragedy?' When terrible things happen in life, you either surrender to circumstance or you meet misfortune head-on and turn things around. I have always sought to instill excellent writing skills and a love of books in my young readers. And I'll continue to do so, which is the purpose of this contest. Whether you believe in the supernatural or not, placing the first contest at Daemon Hall doomed it from the start. This time the finalists will be flown to my home in Pennbrook, New York. My estate,

Tremblin's Lair, may look ghostly, but it is definitely not haunted."

Many in the publishing industry think Tremblin is setting himself up for more legal problems. Others believe he is attempting to turn tragedy into a marketing strategy for his Macabre Master imprint. One unnamed editor at rival Soapstone Publishing has another take. "I'm not the only one who thinks Tremblin should have joined that young writer in the mental institution." The editor is referring to Wade Reilly, a contestant who had to be committed for several months following the first contest. "Tremblin's always been unhinged, and what went on apparently made it worse."

In response, Tremblin commented, "That's a cheap shot at a wonderful young man. Keep in mind that Wade's commitment was due, in part, to a preexisting condition. Wade has been out for months and is faring extremely well. In fact, advance sales for his soon-to-be-released account of what occurred at Daemon Hall are setting records for a first-time author."

Even with a tragic outcome in the first contest, Tremblin as received hundreds of entries from hopeful

PLEASE SEE CONTEST/5D

Article excerpt from the June 15 issue of *Publishing Quarterly*, written by Sharon Sparks, editor for Ian Tremblin's Macabre Master series:

What's amazing is that few in the media take Ian at his word. They think he has some sinister motive for reviving the contest. The simple fact is he truly loves his craft. He's greatly appreciative and respectful of the teens who buy and read his books. He sees the contest as a way to give back to his readership. Yet there is another aspect that I see: the most important thing to Ian is the Story (and yes, I give it proper noun status on purpose). Not only is the Story important, but the Story has to be completed. There is one story that seems unfinished to Ian—what happened that night in Daemon Hall. As is often the case in life versus fiction, the conclusion was far from satisfying, which is frustrating for someone like him. Perhaps with this contest he will be able to bring the Story to a close, and who knows, there may even be a happy ending.

Television Transcript: The Stedman Perspective
Guests: Ian Tremblin, Wade Reilly (show aired July 1)

STEDMAN: I find it hard to believe that any parents in their right mind would allow their children to spend a night with you as part of this so-called contest.

TREMBLIN: Bill, I can understand your concern. This time, however, things will be infinitely safer, simply from the stand-point of locale. There will be no haunted house, no lack of electricity or communication, and other adults—my staff—will be present.

STEDMAN: So what's the payoff?

TREMBLIN: As with the first contest, the winner will have his or her own book, edited by me, published as part of my Macabre Master series.

STEDMAN: I'm talking about *your* payoff, Mr. Tremblin. What do *you* get out of this?

TREMBLIN: I get to promote literacy. I get to interact with my readership, and I'll have the honor of assisting a budding author, just as I did with Mr. Reilly here.

STEDMAN: Really? Some say your payoff is free media coverage. News in the aftermath of your first contest drastically increased your book sales.

TREMBLIN: My motives are not that opportunistic.

STEDMAN: So you say. Let's turn our attention to the winner of your first contest, Wade Reilly. Wade, you've written a book that will soon be released. Supposedly it details terrible things that happened to you in Daemon Hall, yet you're attending again, and your parents are allowing that. Why?

REILLY: They've gotten to know Mr. Tremblin over the past year. They know what happened wasn't his fault. He's helping with my writing career, and they trust him.

STEDMAN: Hmmm. Wade, besides a different locale, aren't there other changes for this second contest?

REILLY: Um, yeah, that's true, Mr. Stedman. As a previous winner, I'll act as a guest judge.

STEDMAN: Interesting. If you didn't have a book coming out, would you still partake in this?

REILLY: I think so, yes.

STEDMAN: Under what circumstances would you *not* participate?

REILLY: There's no way I'd do it if the contest were to take place in Daemon Hall again.

STEDMAN: Not even to promote your book, *Daemon Hall*?

REILLY: Mr. Stedman, let me state for the record that the only way I'd return to that place is if I could somehow destroy it.

Prologue

We enter the house pretending it's no big deal, but I know their hearts are pounding a metalcore drum solo, just like mine. My friend Demarius is tall and skinny with dreads hanging to his shoulders. Kara, the youngest, has black hair and an olive complexion. Chris is a football player with the muscles to prove it. I'm the guy who went crazy and got so scared that my hair turned completely white. We came together because of how much we like to write, so much so that we all entered Ian Tremblin's short story contest and spent the night here.

Terrible things happened.

There are hours of daylight left, yet the windows are black like it's a moonless midnight. We'd have been unable to see if someone hadn't left a lantern on the marble floor at the base of the staircase.

Demarius puts his five-gallon gas can on the floor and picks up the lantern. "Do you think *she* left the lantern for us?"

"Who else?" I say. "It was sitting where she died." Chelsea, like the rest of us, came for the contest. I found her body. Her neck had been broken.

Chris and I put our gas cans down and look around the entrance hall. We stand on the marble floor between the front doors and the grand staircase. We're in Daemon Hall, and it's been exactly a year since that horrible night. I've been many different people since then. There's the Wade who was in the mental institution writing the book, then the healed Wade who was ready to get on with life. The author emerged as I did interviews about my upcoming book. I've also been a vengeful Wade these past few months, plotting with my friends to destroy this place. Now I'm the coward, wishing I hadn't come.

Pressure builds as we hear a noise like rusty hinges on a gargantuan door. The low rumbling rolls through the house, and it's hard to draw a breath. I can't think or reason. I have anxiety attacks, and they scare me, but this generates fear infinitely worse. There's a second of clarity when I see the others are terrified, too. The sound redoubles, and we panic, running in different directions. When the deafening noise stops, I'm in a dark room cowering in a corner. Where is everyone? It comes again. I squeeze my eyes shut, then sense being watched. I look to the door and see two figures. They're hazy and erratic, like flickering images from a damaged reel of movie film.

"Go away!" I cry. "Leave me alone!"

They waver and vanish. Were they ghosts? The Daemons? Maybe others who came and, like Chelsea, couldn't leave.

The sound dies as a dim glow at the open door catches my attention. Have the ghosts returned? It grows brighter until someone stands there holding the lantern.

"Demarius?" I gasp.

"Wade, there you are. I haven't found anyone else."

It begins. The sound. Invisible bands constrict around my chest.

Demarius looks at me with concern. "Wade?"

"The noise," I manage to say, shrinking back into the corner.

"Ignore it."

"What? How?" As it gets louder, I feel more compressed.

"Pretend it's just background noise, like nearby traffic or something."

I start to yell that there's no way, but then I see that he's unaffected. I force myself up.

"That's it," Demarius reassures me. "It's just the house messing with us—ignore it and it won't bother you."

The cacophony is still there, but the fear lessens.

"Yeah, right. It's just noise." Somehow, saying it makes it so and I stand. "Let's find"—it takes a moment to center my thoughts—"Kara and Chris."

We have an idea where one or both of them might be; of all the rooms in the house, there is one that probably feels safest because of familiarity. We discover them hiding behind the desk in the suite that we had used that night one year before. They're scared and hold each other so they won't face the terror alone. We talk them through the process of ignoring the noise, and their fear eases enough that they can function.

"Where's the gas?" I ask.

Chris shakes his head, and Kara looks lost.

Demarius says, "I remember putting down my gas can and picking up the lantern."

Chris rubs his chin. "Yeah, we put them all down in the entrance hall."

Kara's voice shakes. "Then it started. The sound."

"We nearly blew it," Chris says with disgust. "Just because of a stupid noise. Come on, let's finish what we came here to do."

Walking two abreast through the warren of hallways, we turn into a corridor that was not here last year. Where other hallways had once been, there are now walls. The architecture is dizzyingly altered, yet we make it to the great staircase and descend to the first floor and find the four gas cans. We each pick one up, except for Kara, who struggles with the weight.

Chris places the lantern on the floor. "I'll take it. You get ready with these." He passes her a book of matches and picks up her can.

Demarius sloshes gas onto the floor.

"Demarius, don't be an idiot. The floor's marble. Go over there and soak the walls, the furniture, too." Chris points past the stairs to the right. "Wade, get by the door."

Chris and Kara go to the left of the staircase and step into a hallway that resembles a black throat. I splash the wall, several chairs, a settee, a table: everything that isn't stone. Five gallons goes a long way. The fumes make my eyes water as I wait by the lantern. Demarius finishes and drops his can. Chris and Kara emerge from the murky corridor. He has one can left and splashes the wall, moves farther, and splashes more. He comes to a closed set of double doors and douses them. Kara steps away; last year something grabbed her and pulled her through those doors. She's never told anyone what happened during the hours she was missing. She hurries past and stops, watching Chris. He empties the second can and nods at Kara. She pulls a match from the matchbook. Movement catches my eye, and I see the double doors open.

"Kara!"

She turns and sees the hungry darkness beyond the gaping doors. What appears to be a black tree limb emerges. It has no more substance than shadow, yet it moves like a tentacle and whips around her waist, pulling her toward the room. I expect her to scream, but she concentrates on the matches and pulls one over the flint. It ignites. At the threshold she struggles to keep away from the room and what waits within. Kara touches the lit match to the rest of the matchbook, and when it flares, she tosses it against the gas-soaked wall, where it erupts in flame. She's yanked through the doorway, and the twin doors slam.

Flames race along that wall and ignite the doors.

I turn to see Demarius striking a match. "Not yet!" I yell, but he touches off the gas he spilled, which in turn ignites where I'd splashed mine.

Daemon Hall lights up in dancing hues of red, yellow, and orange. Chris and I rush to the flaming doors.

Demarius arrives a moment later. "Let's go!"

The flames have spread, and smoke is filling the entrance hall.

I shout, "Something grabbed Kara!"

Demarius looks shocked and points to the burning double doors. "Again?"

The sense of déjà vu is sickening. "Again."

"Not this time," Chris growls. He backs away and drops into a football stance. A grim determination grows on his face, and he launches himself at the fiery doors. He lowers his shoulder and smashes through, sending one flying from its hinges to crash into the middle of the room. Flames give light to Kara's struggle within a shadowy mass. She frees her right arm and reaches for us. Chris grabs her hand and pulls.

The thickening smoke makes me cough. A little factoid that I'd learned in school comes to me: The majority of deaths in fires are due to smoke inhalation. That's just great.

Chris is pulled along with Kara to another open door. "Help me," he grunts.

Demarius starts after them, but I grab his arm. "Wait."

How can we fight something that is basically insubstantial darkness? With the opposite of dark. I rush to the burning door on the floor. I pick up one heavy end even though flames lick at my hands. Demarius understands and picks up the other side.

"Now!" I shout.

We heave the flaming door through the dark mass behind Kara. The shadow disappears where flames touch it. Chris yanks Kara free, and we run from the room.

The thick smoke blinds us, and the heat is excruciating.

"Which way to the front door?" I yell between fits of hacking.

Nobody answers.

Someone takes my wrist; I can't see who.

"Grab each other!" I shout, and reach my other hand behind me. Someone grasps it—Chris, I judge by the strong grip.

Things detonate in the fire with cracking explosions. The blaze sounds like roaring surf. Whoever has taken the lead pulls us through a maze of smoke and flames. It's hard to keep up; my legs feel like lead, and my lungs are tortured by smoke. I try, I really try to make it, but my knees collapse. In a semi-conscious state, I barely feel pain as I roll down stone steps. My body comes to rest on hard-packed dirt and weeds. I made it out.

Coughing and hacking, we crawl from the flaming structure. Breathing fresh air is painful, yet I suck it in. We all made it,

covered in soot and ash. The fire quickly spreads, and all three stories are ablaze. Flames shoot from windows, black smoke churns into the afternoon air. The outer stone walls withstand the combustion, but inside it's an inferno.

Chris grabs me under the arms and hauls me to my feet. "I can't believe you found the door," he says, pausing to cough. "I was lost in that smoke."

Staring at the fire, I say, "Wasn't me. It was Demarius or Kara."

"No, Kara had my other hand."

"And I was behind Kara," Demarius says from the ground.

I turn to them. "Who led us out?"

Over the fire's roar we hear a prolonged squeak and turn. The distant front gate opens, and a figure passes through, leaving the grounds.

"Who is it?" Kara asks, still wheezing.

The figure stops and looks back at us.

"Chelsea," Chris whispers.

She turns away—and is no longer there.

Subj: Ian Tremblin's writing contest
Date: 11/25 12:03:47 AM Eastern Standard Time
From: Tremblin1@books.net <mailto:Tremblin1@books.net>
To: nanticoke385@earthlink.net <mailto:nanticoke385@earthlink.net>
Received from internet: click here for more information

My dear Ms. Broadwater,

I would like to congratulate you on becoming a finalist in my writing contest. This is quite an honor, as there will be only three finalists competing to win the grand prize: a publishing deal. There will be a small gathering at my estate, Tremblin's Lair, during the Christmas break. On December 20 we will begin the competition, which will continue the following night, December 21. On the morning of the next day, the judges and I will select a winner. Afterward, everyone will return home in time to celebrate the holidays with their families. Reply via e-mail as to whether or not you can join us.

Attached and awaiting download are all the legal documents that you and your parents need to sign and return posthaste. Please make clear to your parents, as I make clear to you, that this is the second contest I have held of this nature. As I am sure you are aware, the first resulted in the unfortunate death of one of the finalists. Be assured that this contest will be conducted in a safe environment. Still, it will be understandable if you or your parents are reluctant to take advantage of this opportunity.

If you do accept this invitation, there is something you must do: write a new story that will be used in the judging of the contest. I provide the title, and you pen the tale. The title of your work is "The Entering."

Good luck and get writing.

Best regards,
Ian Tremblin

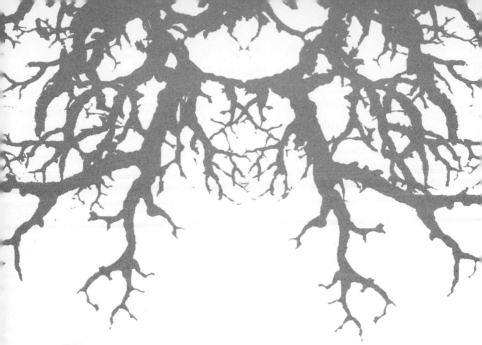

My book had been out since September, and Ian Tremblin arranged a signing at a New York City bookstore prior to my judging his contest. He told me I'd sit at a table, meet a few readers, and sign their copies of *Daemon Hall*. It sounded easy enough. But Ian Tremblin couldn't make it, and his editor, Ms. Sparks, announced that I would also do a reading. I'm not shy, but this was my first trip to New York, and she wanted me to get in front of a bunch of strangers and read from *my* book. What if they didn't like it? What if they started yawning? What if they laughed?

They put me in a smallish room lined with full bookshelves. Book posters covered the walls. A podium stood at one end of the room in front of thirty folding chairs.

"That's all?"

"Hey, only J. K. Rowling gets the auditoriums." Ms. Sparks misunderstood and didn't know I was relieved.

The chairs were filled when it came time to start. Most were kids my age or younger. There were some cute girls, and I thought, *Wow, they came to see me.* Several wore only black. From the mail I'd received, I knew that Chelsea had developed a goth following; she was a hero in their eyes, but then, I felt the same. I read a selection from near the end of the book about the secret candle. When it got to the part where I discovered Chelsea's body, I choked up. I made a mental note that if I did any more readings, I'd pick one of the short stories instead. I was led to a small table and signed books. Most of the people in line asked why Ian Tremblin wasn't there, which knocked my ego back in place.

"Wow! Your hair really is white," one of the cute girls commented.

Some say it's an old wives' tale that terror can turn a person's hair white. I'm proof that it's true.

Afterward, a man in a black suit introduced himself as Anthony, Ian Tremblin's driver. He'd take me the two and a half hours to Pennbrook and Tremblin's Lair. The dry December day was cold, so Anthony cranked up the heater in the big luxury car. The leather seats were as soft as a bed, and I soon fell asleep. When I woke, we were driving through downtown Pennbrook, which sat in a valley, high hills on all sides. There were two- and three-story buildings lining both sides of the streets, mostly merchants and offices. If there'd been snow it would have looked like a quaint village on a Christmas card. A few people were out, bundled up and moving quickly. Anthony made a right and we drove through a section of Victorian homes that perched on small hills.

"Which one is Mr. Tremblin's?" I asked with a yawn.

Anthony glanced at me in the rearview mirror. "It'll be a few more minutes."

We left town and drove through hills and switchbacks. There were a few smaller homes, then nothing but trees towering on each side. Anthony turned onto a gravel road that led through open iron gates and up a twisting drive. We crested a hill, and I got a good look at Tremblin's Lair. It resembled the Addams Family mansion. Though mainly gray stone with black wood trim, there were also white highlights and muted reds. The Victorian home was at least fifty feet high. It had several high, flat roofs. Dormer windows stuck out all over the upper stories. I counted six chimneys. Even though it was winter, I could tell the grounds were well maintained. There were lots of skeletal trees, dormant shrubs, and plants. I imagined the summer landscape was full of lush greens and autumn would unveil dazzling colors.

Anthony stopped at the stone steps leading to the cranberry-colored front door. He got my suitcase from the trunk, handed it to me, and shook my hand. "Have fun, kid." Then he got back into the car and drove around the side of the house.

The house was exactly the kind I expected Ian Tremblin

to live in. A cold gust blew on the back of my neck. I picked up the suitcase and trotted up the steps. Before I knocked, the front door opened and a largish woman beckoned me inside.

"Hello. You must be Wade. I'm Mrs. Rathbone, Mr. Tremblin's housekeeper."

"Pleased to meet you." I shook her hand and, as Mr. Tremblin had once instructed me, observed her in case I needed her description for a future character. She was big-bosomed and sturdy. Her brown hair was touched with gray and collected in a bun. Her face was unlined and pleasant—I imagined that the smile on her lips was pretty much there all the time. She wore a loose green sweater and a white apron.

I'd expected Tremblin's Lair to be gloomy, but the foyer and rooms I could see were painted bright colors. Ample afternoon sunshine came through numerous windows. The foyer was festively decorated with antique Christmas decorations, garlands, and a sprig of mistletoe hanging just inside the door. A staircase with a polished wood banister rose and split in two, one set of stairs going to the left and another to the right.

"I'll show you to your room." Mrs. Rathbone led me upstairs, chatting the whole time. "The furnace runs nonstop in the winter, but it's still cool. Wear a sweater."

"Yes, ma'am."

We took the right staircase and ended up in a bright yellow hallway. Black gas lamps, converted to electricity, were mounted high on either wall.

"That's a portrait of the man who built the home, Everett Billings. He was a railroad baron and had the house constructed in the eighteen hundreds."

We passed a couple of open doors. I peeked in to see pleasantly decorated bedrooms and high beds draped with thick quilts.

"Breakfast is served at eight, lunch at noon, and dinner at eight. If you get hungry in between, help yourself to anything in the kitchen. I know how teenagers can be."

"Thank you."

We stopped at a third room, and she pointed me in. "This is yours. Any questions?"

"Is Tremblin's Lair haunted?"

Mrs. Rathbone's eyes lit up and she laughed, making a dismissive gesture with her hand, then she immediately stopped. "I'm sorry. I shouldn't laugh, considering what happened in Maplewood. No, the only one who haunts these hallways is Mr. Tremblin."

I smiled. "I can handle that."

"Why don't you unpack. I think the others are all in the solarium."

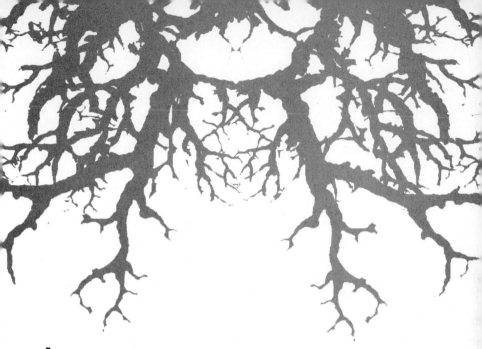

I put my suitcase on the bed and went downstairs. Passing the dining room and kitchen, I followed a hallway with black-and-white-checked tile to a door. I put my ear to it and heard conversation.

At first I couldn't make out any words until a loud voice proclaimed, "It is true."

A flash of recognition hit me, and I flung open the door. "Demarius!"

"Wade!"

Tall, skinny, and wearing a scuffed suede jacket, Demarius crossed the room, dreadlocks swinging, and pulled me into an embrace. "Good to see you, bro."

"You too. I didn't know you'd be here."

"Mr. Tremblin invited me," Demarius said. "He asked Chris

and Kara, too, but they turned him down flat. I'm going to be a cojudge with you."

"So you're two of the judges I have to bribe?" a smiling girl said. She was about our age, and her shoulder-length hair was honey-brown. Like Demarius, she seemed tall; she wore a red sweatshirt emblazoned with BANFF NATIONAL PARK. "I'm Lucinda Taylor, a contestant."

"I'm in the contest, too," another said. She pushed up from a low sofa, and my heart skipped a beat. "I'm Millie Broadwater." She wore a white sweater with tight faded jeans. Her body was fit and curvy in all the right places, and she parted her long black hair in the middle. I found myself drawn to serious brown eyes that angled up at the corners. Her nose was straight and small, her lips full. It took a moment for me to realize she had her hand out.

"Oh, uh, pleased to meet you," I mumbled, and we shook.

"Lucinda is from Alberta," Demarius said. "And, get this, Millie is from Carrolton."

"Carrolton? Really?" The last contest was held in Maplewood, where Demarius and I live. Carrolton was a small town less than an hour from there.

"Yeah. I entered the other contest, too, but didn't make the cut. This time I plan to win and get published. Speaking of which, how's it feel to have a book out?"

"It's pretty cool. I mean, it's at bookstores and all. I did a reading earlier today. But you know what? Even with all that, it still hasn't sunk in."

"You're crazy," Lucinda exclaimed. "If I were published I'd—" She looked at me a moment. "Oh—sorry. I didn't mean you were crazy insane. I meant, uh—"

"It's okay." It sucked that everyone knew I'd been institutionalized.

"Really? Then I'd like to say, wow, your hair is really white."

"Yeah, people keep reminding me." I sat in a deeply cushioned chair and looked around. Windows dominated two walls, stands of plants lined up in front of them. A Christmas tree nearly as high as the ceiling filled the room and was decorated with crystal ornaments, red ribbons, and small white lights.

Millie returned to her seat. "This is so cool, being in Ian Tremblin's house."

Lucinda piped in, "Yeah, I can't wait to meet him."

We laughed, until the lights went out. A resonant voice spoke in rhyme.

> *Be careful who you wish to meet.*
> *You may find he's not so sweet.*
> *The chill you feel will get much colder,*
> *with his hand upon your shoulder.*

Lucinda yelped.

A second later a small light flicked on, a flashlight. It was held by the man we were discussing, the man who had terrorized me one night and had then gone on to mentor me. I smiled as he stood tall and shadowy behind Lucinda, hand on her shoulder.

"Hello, dear," he said, removing his hand. "You must be Lucinda Taylor."

"Mr. Tremblin?" Lucinda was awed. "You scared me."

He turned from her, taking a couple of steps and flipping a light switch. "I apologize, but Wade and Demarius will attest that I like an entrance."

"Oh, yeah," Demarius agreed. "How'd you sneak in?"

"What would Tremblin's Lair be without a secret passage or two?" He pointed to shelves in one of the corners; they'd swung out to reveal a dark passageway.

"Awesome," I said.

"Ah, Wade. Mrs. Rathbone informed me that you'd arrived." He walked across the room and we shook hands.

"I missed you at the signing today."

"I didn't want to distract from what should have been a special day for you." He leaned close and whispered so that only I could hear, "Well done with the fire. I wish I could have been there to see that despicable place go up in flames."

He hadn't changed much. His gray hair was short, his beard was long, and he peered through wire spectacles. He had on a forest green smoking jacket that looked like something Sherlock Holmes would have worn at his Baker Street apartment.

He stepped to Millie and took her hand. "I hope you don't mind my silly antics."

"Not at all," Millie said, smiling.

The solarium door opened and a kid with a thatch of red hair peeked in.

Mr. Tremblin motioned him in. "Allow me to introduce our third and final contestant, Matt Matthews from Tempe, Arizona."

Matt looked ready to bolt, then put on an expression of superiority. He was about twelve and packing too much excess weight. The waist size on his khaki pants was obviously a greater number than the length, and his plaid button-down shirt had an honest-to-goodness pocket protector. I imagined the cutting nicknames he probably endured: Fat Matt, Mammoth Matt, Freckle Face, Pizza Face, the good old standbys dork and nerd. When he opened his mouth to speak, two more came to mind: Metal Mouth and Brace Face.

He pointed at Millie and said, "She's the hot chick." His finger traveled to Lucinda. "And she's the sarcastic girl." He moved on to me. "The returning hero and"—indicating Demarius—"the African-American. Me? I'm the geek. If we follow horror-movie protocol, the first to be killed will either be you," he said to Demarius, "or me."

"Nah." Demarius crossed his arms. "I broke that stereotype last year."

"Besides," Millie said, smiling, "I'm Native American. I might go first."

Matt shook his head. "Nope, hot chick status overrules all others."

Mr. Tremblin sternly interrupted, "No one is dying, Mr. Matthews, nor is anyone to be labeled anything other than writer while in my home. Is that understood?"

Matt looked down. "Sure—whatever."

"Mr. Matthews has numerous talents, including an in-depth knowledge of computers. All morning he's been demonstrating ways to improve my Web site."

"Good to meet you, Matt," Demarius said, and turned to Millie. "You're an Indian? Which tribe?"

"Nanticoke."

Demarius turned to me wide-eyed and whispered, "Oaskagu."

"Oaska-what?" Lucinda asked.

"Oaskagu," I repeated. "The Nanticoke name for the land Daemon Hall was built on. It means dark land."

"Or black land," Millie added.

"I remember," Lucinda said. "That was in your book."

"It was history I'd uncovered while researching Daemon Hall," Ian Tremblin said. "I told them about it during the initial competition. I should have paid closer attention. I would have known not to conduct it there."

Lucinda hiccuped a quick laugh. "It's funny that you guys are still trying to make it sound like Wade's book is true."

"Really," Matt agreed.

Mr. Tremblin rubbed his hands together. "We have dinner reservations in town. I hope everyone has an appetite for fine dining as well as conversation, as we will undoubtedly tackle your disbelief in the evil of Daemon Hall."

We changed into nice clothes. Demarius, Matt, and I were the first ones back to the solarium. Tremblin soon joined us. Ten minutes later, Millie walked in and I couldn't help but stare. She had on a tight violet sundress with stringy straps, which was totally at odds with the weather. To compensate, she carried a heavy down jacket. Her only jewelry was a thin watch on her left wrist. Tan hiking boots were on her feet, and somehow the clunky footwear highlighted her legs, which were downright beautiful. I forced my eyes up and saw her gazing at me, eyebrows raised.

All of a sudden I feared the ol' *why don't you take a picture, it'll last longer* comment, so I blurted out, "You look nice."

She smiled. "Thank you."

Lucinda came in wearing jeans, a fancy blue-checked blouse,

and a gray leather jacket. She'd brushed her cheekbones with glitter.

Demarius and I struggled not to laugh when Matt said, "You have something on your face."

She blew her bangs from her eyes and gave Matt a look that said he was one stupid comment away from being tossed into the Hudson River. This was going to be a fun group to hang with.

We put on jackets, gloves, and hats and stood in front of Tremblin's Lair puffing faux smoke rings in the frigid air. Ian Tremblin announced that we would eat at Amalfi's Crest, his favorite restaurant. Anthony pulled up in a large SUV that had a bumper sticker that read *Cthulhu for president; why settle for the lesser of two evils?*

Lucinda said, "Never heard of that candidate."

Matt, in a snooty, know-it-all fashion, said, "Cthulhu"—he pronounced it KUH-thoo-loo—"is the biggest and most evil of H. P. Lovecraft's monster gods."

Lucinda stared at him.

"The bumper sticker is a joke. It's pretty funny *if* you get it."

Lucinda looked at me and said, "He's obnoxious, but I'm getting fond of the kid."

Amalfi's Crest was a brick building on Main Street. The walls were painted burgundy and were lined with lattices through which plastic grapevines had been woven. Tremblin was greeted by the owner, Antonia, a short, dark-haired woman.

We passed through the kitchen, stopping so she could introduce her husband, Richie, who wore a stained apron and worked in a fog of steam. She led us into a cozy dining room with one table that could easily seat ten.

We removed our winter wear as Mrs. Amalfi bustled about the room lighting candles set in straw-bottomed bottles. She left and came back with drinks and baskets of breadsticks. I like spicy food, so at Ian Tremblin's suggestion, I ordered seafood fra diavolo, a shrimp and scallop pasta dish with a sauce that has its temperature cranked up with freshly crushed peppers.

"Pasta scungilli," Matt ordered with an Italian accent, waving a hand as he said it. It brought a smile to Mrs. Amalfi and made the rest of us crack up. "What?"

"What's a scun-GEE-lee?" Demarius mimicked his pronunciation.

"It's a conch," Matt said with a generous portion of know-it-all attitude.

"A what?" Demarius asked.

"The meat that comes from a conch shell," Millie said.

"Conch, snail, whelk, mollusk, and—most important—delicious!" Matt sat between Lucinda and Demarius. Millie and I ended up next to each other on the other side. Ian Tremblin sat to my right at the head of the table.

Lucinda elbowed Matt. "Pass the breadsticks, Scungilli."

"Matt," he muttered and held the basket as she took one.

"I propose a toast," Ian Tremblin announced, standing and holding up his glass of Chianti. We all stood and did likewise with our drinks. "To our new batch of contestants: Millie, Lucinda, and Scungilli."

Matt tried not to grin at what was probably his first nonmalicious nickname.

"To the new batch." We laughed and took a drink.

"And," Millie said, "to last year's winner, Wade Reilly."

"Hear, hear!" Ian Tremblin echoed.

Millie toasted me? A stupid grin grew on my face.

After the salutations, we sat and Demarius asked, "Mr. Tremblin, I'm working on a sea witch story, kind of a *Blair Witch* in water, and it's just not scary. Why do some things work and others don't?"

"Oh, limitless factors go into what is scary. Much of it has to do with your audience. Serial killers work well because they really exist, and anyone could be a victim. A claustrophobic person would be more terrified of a story about a live burial than someone without a fear of closed-in spaces. Take Wade's book, for example—"

"Yeah, that's terrifying because I was there," Demarius muttered.

"Sure you were." Lucinda nodded mockingly.

Ian Tremblin put up a hand. "I'm referring to the mention of the eighteenth-century English who settled on the land near Daemon Hall and how all the children vanished in one night.

That might be mildly creepy to you whereas, to a parent, it could be downright bloodcurdling. Speaking of scary, how did everyone do with the writing assignment?"

"Good," Millie said. "It was the easiest story I've ever written."

"Really? Me too," Matt added. "Even though your title messed me up at first."

"Those titles weren't from me. I just passed them along."

"Who came up with them?" Demarius asked.

"All in good time," Ian Tremblin said with a smile and a wink.

"When I got mine, 'A Patchwork Quilt,' I wondered how I could make that scary," Lucinda said. "But for some reason it flowed. I like how demented it turned out."

"Hey, Demarius, did you get a title?" I was curious because, even though I was a judge, Ian Tremblin had wanted me to write something.

"Yeah. 'The Go-To Guy.' "

"If Demarius and I are judges, Mr. Tremblin, why do you want stories from us?"

"There were five titles to work with. When you learn where I got them, you'll understand. On the other hand, I love a good story and know that you both can provide entertaining tales." He peeked over his spectacles. "I assigned Wade 'The Leaving.' How did it turn out?"

That was the question I'd hoped to avoid. I've never suffered from writer's block, but when I was working on the story, it was like there was a wall between my brain and the word processor. I spent hours trying but couldn't think of a thing.

Everyone, including Millie, looked at me expectantly. Before I could stop myself, I lied. "It's okay." I tried to change the course of conversation. "So, Mr. Tremblin, are you working on anything?"

"I'm always in the middle of something. Right now it's a novel about a young woman who runs a Web site where people can post videos they take of paranormal experiences. I'm thinking of calling it *Boo-Tube.*" We laughed, and he continued, "Oh, and I've also written a short story for tonight."

"All right! Tell it," Demarius said.

"I was going to wait until later, but perhaps I can relate it before our food arrives."

"Did you get the title from the same place as ours?" Millie asked.

"No. You see, I'm fascinated with the final story I told Wade in Daemon Hall. I don't remember anything that far into the night, so the fact that it was a story I told with no memory of doing so intrigues me."

Lucinda rolled her eyes.

"I know, you think we're making it up, but I don't remember telling it, truly. When I read it in Wade's book, it affected me so much that I wrote a sequel. Actually, it's a prequel."

"Did you bring it?" Matt asked.

The writer shook his head. "No. But I can still tell it to you."

We leaned closer.

"I call it 'To Flee the City of Shadows.'"

TO FLEE THE CITY
OF SHADOWS

There's a small farmhouse, and the first room you enter is a parlor. Picture it in your mind. It's late afternoon, almost dusk, so shadows are thickening. From nearby comes the soft sound of movement. Everything in the room is old-fashioned, from the framed black-and-white photos on the walls to the round wall clock. A large TV is pushed against one wall with two chairs in front of it. One is a lounger; the other is a skinny wood rocking chair. A narrow closet door is underneath a staircase. Next to the closet is this heavy wooden roll-top desk, and on the other side of it is a short hall leading to the kitchen. Two windows, separated by the front door, look out on the front yard.

Ian Tremblin paused a moment, and said, "I know I'm being overly descriptive, but it's important that you have a good idea of what it looks like."

"Go on," Demarius said.

The front door flies open, bangs against the wall, and nearly swings closed. A little girl runs in wearing grubby bib overalls; her tangled blond hair is pulled into pigtails. Breathing hard, she stops to look at the wall clock, then runs to the door and opens it all the way. She hurries to the closet door and twists a lock above the knob, then goes and pulls the chair from the desk, crawls in the chair well, and hides by pulling in the chair.

The clock ticks off a few minutes, and there's a thump followed by a brushing sound. The knob on the closet door rattles, twists, and the door opens. A person emerges. A skinny man in his fifties staggers into the parlor. His neck twists so that his left ear nearly rests on his shoulder. His right arm is drawn up so that his hand dangles under his chin. His left arm swings loosely. He barely lifts his right foot to step, then drags his left behind him. He wears dirty brown slacks, and his T-shirt is stained a crusty brown and rust red. His blank eyes are sickly yellow, and his flesh is the color of ash. He stumbles across the parlor floor and out the open front door, dragging his left foot up and over the sill.

The girl pushes the chair from the desk, crawls out, and runs to the door, shutting it and twisting the deadbolt lock.

"Bye-bye," she says in a sweet little girl voice.

There weren't supposed to be any this far from the city, but we'd spotted four.

"I say we let them catch up, then crack open their heads." Carlos swung a two-by-four.

"No, no, no." Ramsey shook his head. "There's more around, I can feel it."

"Ram's right," I said. "It's night, and we need a safe place."

"Who asked you, loser?" Carlos sneered. He was a big kid with intense blue eyes. He didn't have a drop of Latin blood, but his mom had been a Carlos Santana fan, and that's how he got his name. He was the typical neighborhood bully. Being smaller, I spent my life either avoiding him or getting beat up. It was the same for most of the neighborhood kids, except for Ramsey, a chubby black guy and Carlos's only friend. When it became too dangerous to stay in the city, I left with them.

My old friends might not think much of me running off with Carlos and Ram. They might think of me as a collaborator, something we'd been studying before the breakout. In times of war there are always collaborators, our history teacher had told us. They were traitors who, generally out of fear, worked for the other side. Collaborators in Iraq helped U.S. forces, then passed information to the insurgents. During World War II, collaborators turned in their Jewish friends and neighbors because they were afraid of the Gestapo. Centuries ago, Roman collaborators identified Christians, who were fed to lions in arenas as a form of entertainment. Would traveling with Carlos make me a collaborator?

I'm not sure why they let me go with them. To Carlos I was a weakling, a punching bag that breathed. Maybe on an instinctive level they knew the same thing I did: There's safety in numbers.

"Hey, look at the top of that hill." Ramsey pointed out a small farmhouse illuminated by the moon.

"I don't know if that would be secure," I said.

"Who cares what you think," Carlos growled, and threw the two-by-four behind us. "Maybe they have food." And he started toward the house, Ramsey in tow.

I sighed and followed.

"Hey, it's in pretty good shape," Ram said as we got close.

Shadow Eaters were slow and stupid, but once they got a whiff of fresh meat they were relentless and would shatter windows and break down doors to get people. This place, however, still had windows and a door securely in place.

"A good spot to hunker down," Carlos said.

"If they'll let us," I said.

"Oh, they'll let us," Carlos said, and lifted his shirt for the umpteenth time to display the pistol tucked in his waistband. He'd found it in the apartment of a neighbor who'd been killed when the Shadow Eaters came for dinner. Normally I'd stay away from an armed Carlos, but the way things were then, I liked the idea of a gun in our group. Carlos dropped the shirt and banged on the door. "Hey! Open up! We're living!"

After a few moments, Ramsey tried the knob, but it was locked.

"Get back," Carlos growled, and pulled his pistol.

I guess he was going to shoot the lock, like in the movies. Before he had a chance, there was a soft click and the door opened. It was dark inside, but we saw somebody stepping toward us. Carlos pointed his gun, the barrel shaking, at the figure.

"Are you going to shoot me?" It was a little girl's voice.

Another step forward and we saw a kid in pigtails, wearing OshKosh overalls. Carlos laughed nervously and shoved past her. I followed Ram inside and shut the door. There was no light, and I pulled off my backpack and fumbled for my flashlight. The beam was weak, but it provided something to see by. I pointed it at Carlos, who grinned, knowing my fear of darkness. A match flared and the little girl lit a kerosene lantern that sat on an open roll-top desk. She crossed the room and lit a candle on an old dinosaur of a television, then another on a small table between two chairs.

"Welcome to my uncle's home." There was a trace of a lisp in her small voice. "I'm Melody."

I knelt in front of her. "Hi, Melody." I'd always had a soft spot for little kids. I pointed at my companions. "That's Carlos, and he's Ramsey. My name is—"

"Loser," Carlos said, laughing. "That's *his* name."

She looked at him and said, "You're mean."

Carlos chuckled. "So you better be nice to me, huh? Where's your uncle?"

"He's out getting food."

"If he's out there," Ram said, "he'll be food. We saw numb-munchers."

"He'll be all right. He always is."

Carlos fell into the big stuffed chair. "Hey, loser, your flashlight is dead."

I groaned, not having any more batteries. Since the outbreak in the city, flashlights have become very important. Shadow Eaters can't stand bright lights. In their transition from human to zombie, something happens and they become supersensitive to concentrated light. If the Shadow Eaters forced their way in, I would be without a valuable defense. The lantern and candles wouldn't help; the light they produce is too diffuse.

Someone tugged the flashlight from my hand—the little girl. "We have batteries. I'll put some in for you." She started for the kitchen.

"Hey, brat! Put new ones in mine, too," Carlos ordered.

She got his, then Ram's, and took all three into the kitchen.

Ramsey sat in the rocking chair next to Carlos. "What's the plan, Big C?"

"We'll wait for the uncle to get back with food. If he gives us a hard time, I'll teach him who's boss," he said, patting the gun under his shirt.

"Come on, Carlos," I said. Now that he had a gun, Carlos acted like a gangster.

"Maybe I'll shoot him in the kneecap and throw him out for the numb-munchers."

Ram laughed nervously.

"Don't be a jerk," I said.

I knew I'd said the wrong thing the moment the words came out.

Carlos stood and aimed the gun at me. "You give me any more grief, loser boy, and I'll bust a cap in *your* leg and throw *you* out there. Get this through your head: I can do what I want. Who's to stop me?"

I didn't reply, and he pushed the gun into his pants. Slowly, with my back to the wall, I slid to the floor. Carlos, I realized, wasn't faring too well mentally. Was it the stress of the outbreak, or had he been like that all along? Whichever, I needed to get away before he killed someone, and I'd take the girl.

"Here you go," she called sweetly as she stepped from the kitchen and placed our flashlights on the desk.

"Everyone sit down and wait for her uncle to get back," Carlos ordered, falling back into the stuffed chair.

I stayed on the floor, and the little girl pulled out the desk chair and sat.

Time passed. Carlos and Ram whispered. I slipped in and out of a light sleep. The girl sat quietly, her short legs swinging back and forth.

Carlos kept glancing at the wall clock, and finally stood, moving to the girl. "When is your uncle getting back with the food?"

She giggled. "He went to get food. I didn't say he'd bring any back, silly."

"What?" Carlos's face reddened. "What're we supposed to eat?"

"If you're hungry, there's food in the kitchen. I can fix—"

Carlos grabbed the girl by her bib straps. "You little twerp! I'm starving and you've had food all this time?"

She looked at him, and though tears started to flow, her words were calm and precise. "You're a mean man."

Carlos's face turned red, and he lifted her from the chair. I quickly got up and pulled her from his grasp. Setting her on her feet, I pointed to the kitchen. "You better get Carlos something to eat."

She looked at me gratefully, then turned her attention to Carlos and narrowed her eyes. "Food!" she spat, and marched into the kitchen.

I turned to Carlos and my jaw exploded in pain. I hit the floor, seeing double. When my vision cleared, Carlos stood over me, gun in hand. Had he shot me? I nearly fainted in agony when I touched my jaw. No, he hadn't shot me—he'd hit me with the gun!

Smiling, Carlos turned his gaze to the gun. He had enjoyed that act of violence. Would he like it more if it escalated? He stared at me with glassy eyes, bringing up the gun. There was a flash of light, and I accepted death. Except I wasn't dead.

"What the—" Carlos mumbled.

"Oh, man," Ram said shakily.

Light came through the windows. Not much, just enough so the front of the house was dimly lit. A low-wattage bulb, I guessed. That could be bad, enough light to let the Shadow Eaters know someone is here, but not strong enough to scare them off.

"Who turned that on?" Ram's voice was nearly a squeal.

Carlos ran across the room and pulled down a shade on one of the windows. "Close that one," he ordered Ram.

The little girl appeared in the kitchen hallway, a smile on her lips. This was my chance to get her out. I pushed up on unsteady legs and crossed the room. My jaw still hurt from the pistol whipping, and I was hit with a moment of dizziness. I stumbled against the rocker, which got Carlos's attention. He came at me, then saw the girl standing there.

"Why the hell did you turn on the porch light?"

"Time to eat," she answered matter-of-factly.

"Carlos," Ram said in a forced whisper, "this ain't good."

Shadows were cast against the window blinds. Silhouettes of jerky, shuffling dead. They collected at the windows, first one, then another, then more. I thought they'd force their way in. But no, they simply gathered outside.

Ram hid next to one window, his back flat against the wall. "What do we do?"

Carlos pulled me close and said, "Go get the flashlights."

He shoved me toward the desk and, still light-headed, I nearly fell. I picked up Ram's flashlight, and right away I could tell the weight was wrong. Before I could check it out, Carlos yelled for me to toss it to Ram, which I did. Then I threw Carlos his. I didn't even bother to pick up my flashlight. I knew that it, like theirs, would not be heavy enough.

Carlos moved to the TV set and said, "Okay, here's what—oh, crap, Ram! The girl!"

She stood at the front door twisting the deadbolt. Ram rushed at her as she opened the door. A hand pushed in and grasped his throat. Ram tried to pull away, tugging at the wrist with one hand, banging it with the flashlight in his other. Two more hands reached in; on one of them two of the fingers were just stumps. The stumped hand grabbed his hair; the other tugged at his arm.

"Ram! You idiot! Use the flashlight!" Carlos yelled.

Ram aimed the flashlight through the open door and pushed the button. Nothing happened. I knew why. The girl had taken the batteries out, making them useless. The door banged wide and Ram was pulled into a mass of grasping hands and ripping teeth.

Even before Ram's screams died, the little girl took my hand and led me to the desk. She pulled out the chair and pointed into the chair well, saying, "Get in there."

I got on all fours, crawled in, and sat. As if it wasn't cramped enough, she crawled in, then pulled the chair in as far as she could manage. I sat hunched, head twisted at a painful angle, knees by my ears, and the little girl huddled between my legs.

"We'll be safe now," she said.

"Safe?"

The Shadow Eaters hobbled inside. I could only see what was going on below knee level, which, from my view, showed dirty pants, flayed flesh, and open wounds. Carlos was almost comical, running around like a Chihuahua trapped in a pen with pit bulls.

"My uncle is dead, but he still looks out for me." She spoke calmly. "He came after me a couple of times, but always stopped himself and went outside to hunt instead. I think it's 'cause he loved me lots. Even though he's one of them, some love stayed in him."

I shook my head. I'd never heard of a Shadow Eater passing up food. There were gunshots, and a couple of the numb-munchers stumbled back, then started for Carlos again. The shooting stopped, followed by a couple of clicks, and the gun fell at his feet.

"People leaving the city see our house and how good it looks and come wanting a safe place to stay." The little girl sighed heavily and pointed to the Shadow Eaters' legs. "They leave me alone if I let them in to eat the travelers."

They closed in on Carlos. His flashlight dropped next to his gun. *Bait,* I thought. *They let her live and use her as bait.*

"You didn't have any food or supplies, but most people do— more than enough for me."

She lived off what people left there.

Carlos fell to the floor, his head toward our little hidey-hole. The Shadow Eaters dropped to each side of him like he was a buffet table. He struggled, then lifted his head and saw me crouched under the desk. He didn't plead for help or say anything. Instead, our eyes locked as they began to feed. When one of them, a woman with a badly burned face, bit into his cheek, I closed my eyes and hummed loudly to block the wet sounds.

I don't know if it was shock, the blow to the jaw, or the days and nights of running, but I slipped into unconsciousness. I woke in agony, my jaw swollen and a stabbing pain in my neck from

being twisted in that chair well all night. I crawled out and muttered a good morning to the little girl, who was scrubbing the spot where Carlos had been eaten. There really wasn't much of a mess: What they didn't eat they took with them, and they'd licked most of the blood from the floor. I grabbed a rag and helped her.

Afterward, she led me to the kitchen table and fed me cornflakes and canned milk.

"I'll be leaving soon," I said. "You can come with me."

"No thank you," she answered. "This is my home."

I didn't try to change her mind. Even though she had saved my life, I was glad she turned me down. I recognized her for what she was. Sure, I'd collaborated with Carlos and Ram, teaming up with them to escape the city. But there, sitting innocently on the other side of the table, was history's first collaborator with the walking dead.

"**T**wisted!" Demarius announced with a smile.

Mrs. Amalfi came in balancing numerous plates on her hands and up her arms. As she placed them on the table, everyone congratulated Ian Tremblin on a well-told story, and he grinned like a kid awarded a gold star.

"My mom would point out it wasn't a proper dinnertime story," Lucinda said, "which means I totally liked it." She took a bite of food, and her face melted into a smile.

I tasted my seafood fra diavolo, and it was so good I closed my eyes to savor the flavor. Perspiration beaded on my forehead—oh, yeah, spicy hot! We ate and shared our food. Everything was great, even Scungilli's scungilli. When we started to get full, the conversation turned to the truth, or lack thereof, of what happened in Daemon Hall.

"All I'm saying is I got your book out of the teen fiction section," Lucinda said with a squinted eye.

Demarius, exasperated, sat at the edge of his seat. "It really happened."

Matt shook his head. "Give it a rest, would you? Like Lucinda said, it's fiction."

Demarius started to argue, but Ian Tremblin held up a hand. "How about you, Millie, do you believe?"

She pondered the question. "Well, someone did die. You were in a mental institution." She looked at me with sympathy. "And Mr. Tremblin had legal troubles."

"I know *that* stuff was real," Lucinda said, waving her fork. "But I don't believe in the ghosts grabbing contestants, Mr. Tremblin trapped in mirror-land, oh, and my favorite: the football player sucked down a sink. I mean, come on."

It did sound stupid when put into words; however, Demarius kept arguing. "We were there. We saw. We—we—Mr. Tremblin?"

The writer shrugged.

Millie took a sip of water. "There are strange things out there. But to be honest, it's easier to believe that you suffered some kind of mass hallucination, or you're lying."

"Lying?"

"You get more publicity if people think it really happened."

Demarius, in frustration, flung himself back in his chair.

"There's no argument that will change a made-up mind,

Demarius," Ian Tremblin said. "It would be a different matter if we could take them to Daemon Hall."

"But you can't, since it burned down," Matt countered, and then his eyes lit up. "Hey, if you guys set the fire, like in your book, you'd be in major trouble."

Arson is a serious crime and certainly not something that I should casually confess. I looked to Demarius, but he kept his head down, focusing on the table. Mr. Tremblin, however, gazed at me and gave his head a little shake.

"Well, what about that?" Lucinda asked. "Why weren't you guys arrested?"

Good question, why didn't they lock us up? The answer is simple: because we lied. Before we set the fire, everyone who took part—Demarius, Chris, Kara, and I—agreed that we would keep our involvement secret at all costs. Ian Tremblin was the only one who knew our plans. When the time came, we set up alibis and committed the crime. Mr. Tremblin said that it's sometimes best to hide in plain sight and insisted that I use what happened as a way to end the book.

Of course I can't tell Millie, Lucinda, and Matt all that; instead, I repeated the lie we told the police, the falsehood that kept us from facing arson charges. "When Daemon Hall caught on fire, Mr. Tremblin thought the idea of us setting it would make the perfect epilogue. I spoke with the police and told them I was using a *fictionalized* account of the fire in my book. They couldn't have cared less. I don't think anyone minded that the place burned down."

Lucinda held up her glass and glared at me over the rim. "Hmm, you say the book is true, but now you admit a big part of it is bogus."

Demarius looked miserable. I could tell he wanted to tell them the truth, that we *were* the ones who set the fire. He looked at me and I shook my head. Demarius sighed. "Yeah, well, the rest of the book is true."

Ian Tremblin said, "Anyhow, I liked the epilogue and insisted the publisher add it just before the publication deadline."

"So, the infamous Daemon Hall is ashes now?" Millie asked.

"Naw," Demarius said. "It's a shell of a house. Those stone walls stayed up, but just about everything inside was gutted."

Mrs. Amalfi swept in bearing a tray of something that looked wonderfully sweet.

"Ah, let's continue this later," Ian Tremblin said. "Antonia has brought her marvelous tiramisu! After which we'll return to my house and freshen up. At eleven we'll meet in my favorite room at Tremblin's Lair: the library."

We arrived at the library. Demarius, Millie, Lucinda, and Matt carried their stories in black notebooks that Ian Tremblin had provided. No one seemed to notice that I didn't have one. Ian Tremblin was in his smoking jacket, and the rest of us had changed into lounging clothes.

The library was located in the back of the house and was hexagonally shaped with a high ceiling. Six freestanding bookcases towered over us and radiated from the middle of the room. From above they would resemble spokes in a wheel. They held thousands of books—tens of thousands. The reading area was in the hub and included several plush chairs. A brass plaque was affixed to the end of one of the bookcases. I read it aloud.

BOOKS TO THE CEILING,

BOOKS TO THE SKY,

MY PILE OF BOOKS IS A MILE HIGH.

HOW I LOVE THEM! HOW I NEED THEM!

I'LL HAVE A LONG BEARD BY THE TIME I READ THEM.

—ARNOLD LOBEL

Demarius laughed. "You already have the beard, Mr. Tremblin."

"Didn't Arnold Lobel write the Frog and Toad books?" Millie asked.

"Yes, indeed."

"I loved those when I was a kid."

Smiling, Ian Tremblin said, "I still do. In fact, I'd love to have that poem on the home page of my Web site. We'll need permission and to attribute it to Lobel, of course."

"I'll take care of it when we're done," Matt said. "What's the password to get into your Web site utilities?"

Tremblin looked at everybody. "I'm sure I can trust all of you. It's *Afghanistan banana stand.*"

Matt snickered. "Not likely to forget that."

Millie grinned. "Afghanistan banana stand—rolls right off the tongue."

Demarius laughed, then his smile faded when he looked to the center of the room where a pedestal stood. Next to it was something both familiar and unsettling: the candelabrum Mr. Tremblin had brought to Daemon Hall for the first contest.

Demarius eyed it warily. "I can't believe you went back for that."

"Not until it was morning. I was helping the police search for Wade, and after we checked the study, I went ahead and took it with me. There's a sentimental attachment."

He turned and held out his hand, indicating the hundreds of volumes on one of the bookcases. "These are collectibles: first editions, antiques, rarities, that kind of thing." Some were bound in cloth, others in leather. Some titles were written by hand and some used gold leaf. There were those that looked ancient and ready to fall to pieces, and others, while obviously old, were in excellent shape. "Please don't touch these, they're easily damaged. This room is climate-controlled for their preservation."

"Here's the good stuff." Demarius stood before another bookcase. "Neil Gaiman! Here's Stephenie Meyer and Garth Nix. Scott Westerfeld anyone?"

"Perhaps later, Demarius. Now is the time to show all of you what will be the most important book during our contest." Ian Tremblin led us to the pedestal in the middle of the library. "Wade, examine this, please."

The volume on the pedestal was the size of an unabridged dictionary and covered in cracked brown leather. At first I thought it was without a title, but I looked closer and saw faint brown smudges that were nearly invisible letters.

"Try this." Mr. Tremblin handed me a large magnifying glass.

I bent over the book deciphering the title letter by letter. I felt a cold jolt and the little hairs on the back of my neck stood on end as I lifted my gaze to the others.

"What is it?" Millie asked.

Smiling, Ian Tremblin said, "I've always believed that a good book transfers the reader to another place and time. I think Wade is experiencing a similar sensation."

"What's the title?" Demarius asked.

I took a deep breath and told them, "*Book of Daemon Hall.*"

Demarius groaned. "Aww, I thought we were done with that place."

"No worries, Demarius, we won't leave Pennbrook." Ian Tremblin turned to me. "Yours is not the first book on Daemon Hall, Wade. See for yourself."

I touched the book. Though it sat in a cool, climate-controlled room, the cover felt warm, like flesh.

"Open it," Millie said impatiently.

I cautiously turned to the first page. At the top was an illustration of a skull. Two crossed pens were drawn underneath, the kind you have to dip into an inkwell. Below those were handwritten words, one over the other.

"Titles?" Lucinda asked.

"Looks like it." I read them aloud. " 'The Entering,' 'A Promise for Bones—' "

Matt interrupted, "That's the title you gave me, Mr. Tremblin."

" 'The Go-To Guy,' 'A Patchwork Quilt,' and 'The Leaving.' "

Demarius looked from the page to Ian Tremblin. "A table of contents?"

He nodded. "I gave each of you, judges included, a title to use in developing a short story. They were taken from this book."

Matt picked at his face. "Why write stories for titles that already have stories?"

I turned to where the first story should start, but other than the title, the page was blank. I flipped through until I got to another title, but still no story.

"Have a seat for a history lesson on the *Book of Daemon Hall*."

We got settled, everybody else putting their notebooks by their chairs.

"After the publicity of our contest last year, I was contacted by a book dealer who claimed to possess a volume entitled *Book of Daemon Hall*. This was over eight months ago. Since then I've learned little."

"I'm surprised you could find *anything* about an old book like that," Millie said.

"Via the internet, I discovered that the Daemon family historical papers are archived at the University of Chicago; the school was founded by John D. Rockefeller, who partnered with Rudolph Daemon's father on various business ventures. The Daemons made substantial donations to the school, which is why their family papers are kept there. At the university I learned the history of the home's construction. Millie, as a Nanticoke, you're aware of the legend of Oaskagu, the black land upon which Daemon Hall was built."

"Anyone who read Wade's book knows about that," Lucinda said.

Millie nodded. "It's Nanticoke lore. In fact, Oaskagu is the setting for my story."

Ian Tremblin widened his eyes. "Really?"

"When I sat down to write, it seemed the only possible locale. What I know about Oaskagu comes from my grandfather."

"A historian of your people?"

"My great-great-grandmother was the last person who could fluently speak the Nanticoke tongue. His interest started with her, and he kept gathering knowledge until he knew more about Nanticoke history than just about anyone."

"Let's see what he taught you." Ian Tremblin focused on Millie and spoke slowly. "There was a tree where Rudolph Daemon located his home. This tree, on the dark lands, was described as towering, black, and—unique."

Millie leaned forward in her chair. "That's funny."

"Funny strange or funny ha-ha?" Demarius asked.

"Funny interesting. Oaskagu's evil supposedly came from a spirit that either lived in or took the shape of a giant tree, what they called Oaskaguakw, or dark tree. I'm wondering—could those two trees, Daemon's and the Nanticokes', be the same?"

Lucinda rolled her eyes. "You talk like all this is real."

"This is history, Lucinda. It plays into the Daemon Hall estate, a place some of us have experienced." Ian Tremblin spoke forcefully. "You don't believe, fine, but you can't deny history. Rudolph Daemon had the tree cut down and pulped some of it. It was turned into paper, from which he had that made." He pointed at the *Book of Daemon Hall*.

"No offense," Matt said, "but what's the big deal about a blank book?"

"We all know the fate Rudolph Daemon suffered, right?"

"Oh, yeah," Demarius said. "He went nuts and killed his family."

"His madness started about the time he had the book made to chronicle the history of Daemon Hall. Yet he claims never to have written in it. The book, according to him, filled itself with insane histories of the surrounding land." Seeing our puzzled expressions, he spelled it out for us. "Rudolph Daemon claimed that the book wrote itself."

"Ha! Give me a break," Lucinda exclaimed.

"I'm just telling you what Rudolph Daemon thought." The writer shrugged.

We were quiet until Demarius said, "I'm confused. Nothing's in the book except for the titles. If it *wrote* itself, where are those stories?"

"Obviously there were no stories. The pages are and have always been blank, but to Daemon, a man in the throes of madness, it appeared to be filled with historical accounts of unimaginable horrors. I believe, in his mental state, Rudolph put those titles in and imagined anything else he saw written there."

"So, besides a contest, you'll put our stories in the book?" I asked.

"Yes, which will keep the unsettling spirit of Daemon Hall in our competition without our actually having to go there. I had you write stories based on the titles in the book. Millie, Lucinda, and Matt will be judged on those entries. The winner, like Wade in my last contest, will have a book published in my Macabre Master series. And though Wade and Demarius are judges, they will tell stories based on the other two titles."

I squirmed in my seat. The pressure from not writing a story was turning out to be about a hundred times worse than any homework I'd ever neglected.

"After the contest everyone's story will be handwritten into the book. Why? you may ask. Because there's nothing more pathetic than an unfinished book, especially one with the frightening potential of this one. Millie, you were assigned the first title, 'The Entering.' Please do us the honors."

Millie picked up her notebook from the floor and carried it to the pedestal, where she placed it on the open pages of the *Book of Daemon Hall*.

"Hold on." I went over to the Día de los Muertos candelabrum, what had been our sole source of light during that night in Daemon Hall. It was made of black metal with candles mounted at the top on a slanted S shape held up by interwoven bars. El Día de los Muertos means "the Day of the Dead." It's a Mexican holiday, in honor of which several pottery objects had been imbedded in the framework: skulls, skeletons, and coffins. Two matchbooks sat on a lantern at the base of the candelabrum.

"Turn out the lights," I said to Demarius.

"Excellent idea, Wade," Ian Tremblin noted.

I waited for full darkness, then struck a match and lit the candles. Shadows flickered over our faces. We could just make out the freestanding bookcases and nearby chairs, but the rest of the library had been swallowed in gloom.

I glanced from Lucinda to Matt to Millie. "In Daemon Hall we learned that some things are best read by candlelight."

THE ENTERING

There was a proud people known as the Kuskarawaok, who lived south of the great Iroquois Nation, north of the Tuscarora tribe, east of the Lenape and Munsee, and southwest of the island-dwelling Wampanoags. Because they flourished along the rivers near the sea, they were called Nantego, meaning tidewater people. When Captain John Smith arrived, their name was anglicized into Nanticoke. Their numbers dwindled in the early 1700s, and by the 1800s the tribe was close to extinction. But for a handful of words, the language is forgotten, and when words are lost, stories fade like vague dreams. Even so, there is a tale that is still handed down from one generation of Nanticoke to the next.

Leaves crunched under my feet as I hurried through the forest. A full moon turned forest colors of green and brown into hues of blue and gray. I ran as Father taught me. *"Place your eyes ten paces ahead, so that when you reach where your eyes have been, your body will know how to go."* When the growth got too thick, I attempted Father's more difficult instruction: *"Use your mind's eye to see that to which you are blind."* I slid through the woods quickly and fought the desperate urge to look behind, for that would slow me, and if I slowed, I would join Father in death.

Little Fox, like her name, was small and solitary. She had somber, dark eyes and black hair, some of which was braided while the rest fell down her back, and she wore leather leggings and a breechclout instead of the knee-length skirt of Nanticoke women. The boys liked to tease her, saying she wanted to be a man, but the truth was she longed to be a warrior. Girls couldn't train with the boys in the skills of fighting and the hunt, but her father, Silent Wolf, respected her need and taught her the use of the bow and war club. She and her father were close, even more so since her mother had died in sickness.

The Nanticoke hunted, fished, and farmed. They were competitive and enjoyed athletic contests. Wars were rare, and it was a serene and peaceful existence for the most part—except when they were plagued by a monster. Off and on throughout her people's history, a great beast terrorized the Nanticoke. It had recently returned and was thought to live in the thick forest and wet marshes of Oaskagu, the dark land.

Little Fox had been upset when her father went to hunt the beast and left her at home.

"But Raging Bear goes with you," she argued, "and he is my age."

Her father laid a hand on her shoulder. "Raging Bear is already taller than any man in our village. He has mastered the ways of the warrior and goes to prove his courage."

Though Raging Bear was strikingly handsome, Little Fox disliked him. He was egotistical and antagonistic, traits the adoring village girls overlooked. Her dislike also contained a degree of jealousy, as she was competitive by nature and he beat her at every contest: wrestling, racing, and archery.

So, it angered her that Raging Bear joined the hunt for the great beast, along with her father, Proud Antelope, and Moss Back, but it devastated her when Raging Bear was the only one to return.

Her tribe's leader, a weathered, white-haired warrior named Four Winds, called for a gathering. Little Fox was allowed to attend, as were the wives and daughters of the other hunters, in what was normally a men-only meeting lodge. The drummers beat their cadence, and the fire pit blazed. Raging Bear was led in. Black tattoos were on each arm; lines like waves encircled his biceps, and on each forearm was his namesake, the bear. He shuffled to the fire and plunged both hands into the coals, then pulled them out and used his fingertips to draw parallel lines of ash down his cheeks. He set his jaw and told of what happened.

"Four of us set out. The first sign of the beast was at the Quiackeson." The Quiackeson was the small lodge used in the first stage of burial. "The door was broken, and the remains of Old Wolf and High River had been ravaged by the beast. We returned the dead to dignified rest and went into Oaskagu. The beast came from behind and took Proud Antelope."

A shriek filled the lodge, and Shining Flower, Proud Antelope's woman, collapsed to the earthen floor. At a gesture from Four Winds, she was taken from the lodge.

"We gave chase until the trail disappeared. We each went a different direction. I'd not gone far when I heard a shout and the sounds of battle, so I ran back to find spilled blood. What killed my brother warriors had dragged their corpses away. I followed the bloody trail, but it ended at Oaskaguakw, the black tree."

Little Fox hated him for not searching more, and as tears tracked her cheeks, she realized she hated him doubly for being the last person to see her father alive.

It was hard to ignore the pain in my side and keep running, but in my training Father once said, "A warrior's strength starts here," and tapped my head. "It is here that you defeat pain and exhaustion."

Like a following wind, the beast called, "Wait for me, Little Fox. I will be loving and will whisper your name as I devour your flesh."

A Lenape warrior visited the village to say they too were hunted by the beast. "It took warriors, the elderly, and the young. We learned that it hunts only when the moon hangs full. On those nights we stay safe in our wigwams. None have been taken since."

The Nanticoke then, like the Lenape, stayed secure in their wigwams on those full-moon nights, and no more were lost.

Time passed. Soon the boys her age would prove their courage and become warriors. Usually they were given grueling tasks or sent on long journeys, but fate provided a different opportunity. Mohawks had raided a Nanticoke village to the north. The warriors of the five villages of the Kuskarawaok River, including the boys she had grown up with, would make an answering attack of war to the Mohawks. She desperately wished to be included.

The warriors gathered at dusk in the meeting lodge for the war council. Little Fox snuck inside and stayed back in the shadows, but Four Winds had keen eyes.

"Hello, Little Fox. Have you come to wish us well?"

She stepped forward and said, "I will join those my age and go into battle."

The others laughed, but Four Winds was fond of her and held up his hands for silence. "Little Fox, I know your courage exceeds your size, but you cannot join us in war." He smiled warmly at her. "You are a girl. Girls become wives, not warriors."

Flushed with anger, Little Fox left the lodge, wandered from the village, and came to sit on a rock in a stream. It was the night of a full moon, when the beast hunted, yet she didn't care. Her thoughts were of the Mohawks. How could she prove herself to Four Winds and the village council?

"Oaskagu."

She heard the word and looked up to see Raging Bear on the

bank. She stood as he walked into the water and stopped several paces from her. "I am here because I respected your father, Silent Wolf. He was a great warrior. If I had been faster or stronger, then he might still live." Raging Bear splashed to the rock and sat at Little Fox's feet. "I wish to help you."

Amazed, Little Fox sat at his side and asked, "How?"

"Oaskagu. If we go to Oaskagu and return with the carcass of the great beast, how could they say you are not a warrior and not allow you to join our war against the Mohawk?"

"Why do you help me?"

"I failed your father, and in so doing I owe his daughter."

"When?" she asked.

Raging Bear smiled. "Now. The moon is right. Go prepare. I will meet you here."

Several times I thought it possible that I had lost my pursuer, but would then hear the beast call out and taunt me. Without weapons, I realized I would probably die there in Oaskagu. But another of Father's lessons came to mind. "No matter how hopeless a situation, there is always a chance to emerge victorious." I thought of something that offered the most meager of hopes.

Back in her wigwam, Little Fox shaved her head into a scalplock, one long lock of hair that warriors wear into battle. Manito, the good spirit, was said to fly through the woods unseen. So too would Little Fox. She collected ashes and mixed them with berries and water into a thick black paste and drew designs of forest shadow across her body.

Little Fox loaded her father's prayer pipe with tobacco. Women did not smoke, and if caught, her punishment would be severe. Sitting before the fire pit in the center of the wigwam, she lit it with an ember. With her first puff, she prayed for the swiftness of the eagle's wing. On her next draw, she prayed for the strength of the cougar. With each inhalation, she prayed for the things Manito could provide—stealth of the serpent, agility of the squirrel, protection of the turtle's shell—until the pipe was spent. She took up her bow and arrows and grabbed her heavy wooden war club. Outside, she ran silently through the village into the forest and joined Raging Bear, following him toward Oaskagu.

There were many tales of the dark land passed around campfires, like the one told by Broken Feather, who'd been setting traps near there when he saw a black stag. He said that its antlers did not grow from the top of its head but from its eye sockets.

"It had no trouble seeing," Broken Feather had said in a whisper, "because each antler ended with a round, wet eyeball."

At the border to Oaskagu, Little Fox sang a prayer of safe passage to Manito.

Raging Bear snorted and said, "Prayers will not help in there." He leaned against a tree and looked at her for a long moment. "It amuses me to see you this way. A scalplock and arrows do not make you a warrior. You are a girl, Little Fox. When you become a woman, your place should be next to a man."

"Then why hunt with me?" Little Fox spat.

Raging Bear repeated, "I failed the father and owe the daughter." He watched her a moment, then said, "You have fire in your spirit." He walked past her into Oaskagu and stopped to add, "Is it enough to keep you alive?" He disappeared into the thick woods.

She followed, and the moment she stepped over the invisible boundary, she felt corruption rising from the ground. Little Fox unslung her bow and notched an arrow.

My sense of direction is good, and I worked my way to the right so that I would eventually run in a circle that returned me to where the chase started.

Raging Bear led them into a clearing. In the center, in front of the full moon, stood a monstrous tree.

"Oaskaguakw," he said, gazing at the tree in wonderment.

The bark was as black as obsidian. It was taller than the tallest pine with a trunk wide enough to hide ten warriors. Each limb, shrouded in dark moss, ended in a sharp point. A thick odor of decay surrounded the area.

Raging Bear, gazing at the tree, said, "The beast no longer eats the dead."

"What?"

"It eats only the living."

"I don't understand."

"The beast was a carrion eater, a scavenger that fed mainly on those already dead. But something changed, and it began to hunt the living Lenape. The Lenape learned when it hunted and cowered in their villages on those nights, so the beast began to take prey from our village. The Lenape shared their knowledge with us, and the beast turned to the Munsee. The Munsee, too, realized that it only hunts on the full moon and have secured themselves. The other tribes are much too far for the beast to reach in one night."

"It has lost its prey?"

He didn't answer, but said, "I lied to the village. Here is what really happened to your father." Raging Bear leaned his weapons against the black tree, then sat cross-legged. Little Fox, confused, sat and placed her weapons within reach. He looked into her eyes and spoke. "Proud Antelope was the first killed. That left three of us—Silent Wolf, your father; Moss Back; and me. We followed the trail. At the base of Oaskaguakw, the black tree, we found much blood. We heard laughter from up high. The beast dropped Proud Antelope's dead body onto your father and leapt onto Moss Back."

Little Fox leaned forward. "What—what is it?"

"A man," Raging Bear said. "He seemed not much older than us. His eyes glowed like a night animal, and his skin was green, like leaves. He slashed at Moss Back with his fingers, and blood flew."

"He kills with his fingers?"

"Longer than a man's, claws on each. The skin around his mouth hung loosely and yet his lips snarled back like a dog's. His teeth were sharp with a space between each. He glanced at me and saw I was too frightened to fight. So instead of coming for me, he buried his teeth into Moss Back's throat. He lifted his head and smiled at me through a gore-smeared face, then chewed and swallowed the meat he'd taken."

Little Fox shivered. "What of my father?"

"He struggled to free himself from underneath Proud Antelope's corpse, but the falling body had broken many of his bones. The beast—the man—dropped Moss Back and started toward your father, who managed to sit up and notch an arrow onto his bow. He let fly and struck the man-beast directly in the heart. The man-beast remained standing with the feathered shaft protruding from his chest! What strength!"

"Did you—did you help my father then?"

Raging Bear's eyes were wide with excitement. "No, Little Fox. I ran. I ran until the old man blocked my path."

"Old man?"

"He came from nowhere, and I screamed like a . . ."

"Coward," Little Fox finished.

" 'Surely I didn't scare you?' the old man said. 'Are you not courageous?' In that moment I felt shame.

" 'Do not worry,' the old man said, knowing my thoughts. 'You will be a great warrior.' Frail, he gazed at me with rheumy eyes. His ribs pushed against his flesh. Hair the color of dirty snow hung tangled about his head. Half his nose had been rotted by disease. Your father's arrow still pierced his chest."

Little Fox gasped. "But you said the man-beast was young and strong."

Raging Bear didn't explain, but continued, "I tried to speak in a harsh tone but could only whimper, 'Who are you, grandfather?'

"The old man laughed. 'Me? I am not you, but you will accept me.'

"He beckoned me to follow, and we came to a clearing in which a fire burned. He sat on a rock and put a long pipe to his lips. I sat on a log across the fire. The old man gazed at me and drew on his pipe. Smiling, he exhaled and reached through the fire, ignoring the flames on his flesh, and handed me the pipe.

"'This is special tobacco. Close your eyes and empty your lungs. Take as much smoke as you can.'

"Slowly I inhaled. I peeked through my lids and saw the old man reach across the fire. His arm turned to black smoke—and I sucked it into the pipe. It stung my throat. The old man's shoulders and head changed, hung in the air, then followed his arm into the pipe. Finally my lungs were full and I exhaled, though no smoke accompanied my breath. I opened my eyes and saw the old man, now only body and legs, turn to smoke and drift over the pipe bowl. I breathed in the rest of the man-beast."

Little Fox watched him suspiciously. "Are you the old man?"

"I am tradition, one that was born in Oaskagu. Before our fathers' fathers, a flesh eater came to be. Our ancestors called him the beast. Though he fed mainly on dead flesh, he would take a live body when there were no dead."

"How do you know this?"

"I took his knowledge. The beast was away for several

generations, hunting in the far north, before returning. Your father's arrow killed him. But flesh eaters are strong, and death comes slowly. Mortally wounded, he passed from his youthful strength into that dotty old man. At the fire I witnessed his death, where he passed the custom of eating flesh to me." Raging Bear beat his chest as if it were a great honor.

Little Fox rose from sitting to squatting, hoping Raging Bear wouldn't notice.

"Until a flesh eater receives a true death blow, like an arrow through the heart, he is immortal. He has the strength of ten warriors and the speed of the hawk. The old man chose me to carry on. I sneak from the village on the full moon and become the beast."

"Why are you not satisfied with the dead? Why do you hunt the living?"

Raging Bear smiled as if he'd been caught doing something naughty. "I am supposed to be a scavenger. My first meal as a flesh eater should have been the dead, and in so doing the dead would have become what I sought. But if the first meal is living flesh . . . ?"

Little Fox gagged.

"I know. It is wrong. I feel shame after I eat and vow to do it no more. But as the full moon approaches, the urge gets strong, I remember how good it feels—tastes. So I tell myself, *Just once more, then I'll quit.* But no, the craving overpowers my will." He wore a look of unfathomable sadness, then a smile came to his lips and he jumped up and ran to the black tree. "The remains of your father are here," he said, rubbing the bark.

"In the tree?"

"When hunting near Oaskagu, all the man-beasts discarded the remains of their prey into Oaskaguakw. See where the first great limbs separate?" He pointed to a high spot where a dozen or more thick limbs branched off. "That is where a hole opens into the trunk and where we toss what is not eaten. This is your father's Quiackeson."

Little Fox's rage ignited. "You ran like a child while the beast killed my father."

"The beast let your father live."

Little Fox gasped. Her voice quavered as she asked, "The beast didn't kill him?"

"I returned to your father as he freed himself from underneath Proud Antelope's body." Raging Bear closed his eyes and smiled. His auburn skin shifted to a pale green. His hands twitched as black claws extended from lengthening fingers. "My first meal as a flesh eater was of the living. I am spoiled and cannot stomach *dead* flesh." His eyes opened. "I fed on the father and now hunger for the daughter."

Little Fox ran, stumbling when she realized she'd left her weapons behind.

Raging Bear laughed. "Don't run. Join your father in my belly."

It had been many miles, and the chase returned to Oaskaguakw. I was fatigued and could only lope into the clearing where my weapons lay. A root of the dark tree rose from the ground and it tripped me. I fell hard, skidded, and lay there a moment gulping air.

After resting, I crawled to my weapons and the clearing filled with a warbling howl. Rolling onto my back, I gripped the bow in one hand, an arrow in the other. My vision dimmed as I sat up, and I struggled to stay conscious. When my sight cleared, I saw Raging Bear approach like a charging grizzly. He ran on all fours, clawed hands digging into the ground and throwing up clumps of dirt. The chase had weakened me so that my bow seemed as heavy as stone. Still I raised it and tried to aim, but he moved too fast, and my exhausted arms shook. I am ashamed to say that I sobbed like a child.

Father spoke then. Not a memory—his actual voice came from the black tree: "Little Fox, you have to act quickly and accurately—or die."

I unleashed the arrow.

Four Winds sat unmoving. Those gathered in the meeting lodge kept a respectful distance. Raging Bear's weapons lay between them on a blanket. She had told her people the story, described how angry Raging Bear had become when the arrow pierced his heart.

"NO! I am to live a hundred lifetimes as the greatest flesh eater!" With the arrow in his chest, he ran at me. I dropped the bow and scooped up my war club. When Raging Bear got close, I turned as if to flee, but instead I spun around, and with all the strength that

I possessed, I smashed the club into the beast's knee. *Raging Bear* fell. I swung again and crushed his head.

Falling to the ground, I cherished each breath while enduring cramps in my sides and legs. Finally, I got to my feet and looked down at Raging Bear. He had a punctured heart and crushed skull, yet breathed. Our eyes locked and then he vanished. His breechclout and leggings collapsed on empty space. Black smoke floated where his body had been. The cloud drifted toward me, and though exhausted, I had to run yet again. I tried hard, but my pace slowed until I stumbled through the woods. When I looked back, it was directly behind me, reaching out a tendril. It touched me, an obscene tickle on my neck, then I was past the dark land, out of Oaskagu, and I fell to the ground. The smoke stopped at the border and dissipated into nothing.

Four Winds gazed upon her. "You returned with Raging Bear's weapons but not your own. Why?"

"After the smoke scattered, I returned to Oaskagu. At the black tree I dug a hole and buried my weapons. I sang a prayer that they be preserved should a warrior ever need them to fight the Oaskagu evil. I would have brought Raging Bear's head to prove my story, if he had not turned to smoke. I brought his weapons instead."

Four Winds stood and addressed the assembly. "When a warrior falls in battle, his memory is honored by the care of his weapons." He tossed the club into the fire, and broke the arrows and bow. "No such honor shall come to Raging Bear." Pulling Little Fox to her feet, Four Winds faced the tribe. "From this day forth, Little Fox is no more. She is Fox Warrior Woman—and she will lead our warriors against the Mohawk."

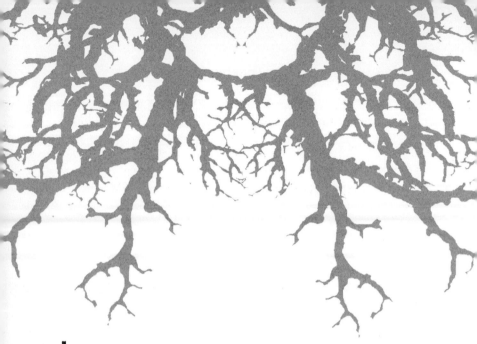

Ian Tremblin gave Millie an appreciative nod.

"That was great," I said.

Lucinda blew at her bangs, something I'd come to recognize as a sign of anger or frustration. "Did you help with her story, Mr. Tremblin? I mean, you have a book supposedly made from a black tree, and a black tree pops up in her story."

Ian Tremblin held up his hands and laughed. "The only help I gave Millie was the title. The fact that she used the black tree is totally coincidental."

"It's always been a Nanticoke legend, Lucinda," Millie said.

Smiling, Tremblin said, "You're a suspicious one, aren't you?"

She shrugged. "Mom says I have all the bad qualities that begin with *s*: suspicious, sarcastic, and cynical. One of these days I'll point out that cynical begins with a *c*, but right now it's my private joke."

"Well, it brings up a good point. Any mentions of the black tree in other stories?"

Matt slowly held up his hand. "There was a tree."

"Oaskaguakw is in your story, too?" Millie asked.

"No, not anymore. And it was just a tree, not Oaska-ga-whatever."

"What do you mean *not anymore*?" Ian Tremblin asked.

"I took it out. The story was turning out great until I started writing about a tree making people sick, which seemed kind of stupid, so I took it out."

Demarius lifted his nose. "Those candles give off a lot of smoke."

The writer sniffed. "Yes, though I enjoy their ambience."

"And it feels weird, doesn't it? Like something—I don't know—isn't right."

The candles flickered as motes of dust twirled above the flames, which I thought odd, considering this was a climate-controlled room.

"I feel it, too." Matt stood and looked around.

"I assure you that—" An expression came to Tremblin, one I recognized from when things started to get weird in our first contest: expectation combined with anxiety.

Lucinda stood. "Something's burning."

"Just the candles," I said.

"Perhaps Ms. Broadwater's story has shifted our imaginations into overdrive. A short break might be in order. Would someone get the lights, please?"

Demarius pushed up from his chair and walked into the darkness. After a moment, there was a crash and he cursed.

"Are you okay?" I called.

"I tripped." Demarius stepped into the candlelight. Black and gray dust covered his hands and forearms, and collected in his dreads. The knees of his pants looked like he'd crawled through a fireplace. "I went to where the lights are—or should be." Demarius looked at me. "I tripped over a burned piece of wood and fell in a pile of ash."

We stared dumbly at Demarius until Millie gasped, pointing at the *Book of Daemon Hall*. We crept closer. It was opened to two pages filled with words. Ian Tremblin examined it closely, and his expression went from awe to apprehension.

"Marvelous—incredible—frightening."

Lucinda and Matt, rookies at this kind of thing, thought it was a trick.

"Wow, Mr. Tremblin! How did you do that?"

"That's creepy, like something out of a movie."

Millie looked at the open pages. "It's *my* story, written in here."

I studied it. "Is that your handwriting?"

"Not even close."

Demarius and I gave each other a horror-struck *not-again*

look. He grabbed my shirtfront and pulled me close. "I can't do this, Wade. Not again."

I grabbed his wrists and made him release me. "Don't freak, okay?"

"Freak? Of course I'm freakin'." He picked up the lantern and stuck a candle inside. "We're in—" But he didn't finish. Circling us, he illuminated the chairs and podium from Ian Tremblin's library.

"Where are the bookcases?" Lucinda asked in a hushed voice.

Demarius went farther, the lantern showing us a room that had suffered a fire. An inside wall was gone; another had gaping holes in it. Charred lumber, ash, and debris covered the blackened marble floor. Night sky was visible through holes that had burned through the floors and ceiling overhead.

Ian Tremblin put a hand over his face and, oddly enough, began to giggle. He tried to stop, but couldn't. "We began—the story in my library, and we—and we—ended the story in another several hundred miles away." His giggles turned to laughter.

Was this something I'd witnessed before, something bad? He waved his hand as his laughter subsided and started again, then he swallowed. "I'm sorry, I'm really"—he paused to snicker. "I'm afraid I was blindsided by—um—a case of nerves, really." He chuckled one last time and took the lantern from Demarius. "We're in the first-floor library, or where it used to be before the fire. Several rooms up that way"—he pointed—"is where Kara was taken."

Lucinda hugged herself like she was cold and gaped into the surrounding gloom. "You're saying we're in Daemon Hall, aren't you?"

Demarius's voice quavered. "Didn't believe us, huh?" His eyes were crazy. "Welcome to the nightmare! For the record, every word of Wade's book is true."

"So it really happened?" Lucinda fell into a chair. "You even set the fire?"

"Of course," I snapped. "We lied because police don't particularly like people setting homes on fire, even if they are old, abandoned, and haunted." I sat, my irritation gone. "We had to destroy it." I put my head in my hands. "We failed."

In an instant, my heartbeat escalated. I could feel it pound in my temples and squeeze my brain. Right away I knew this could be the strongest panic attack I'd had since I'd been in the hospital. When my breaths turned shallow, I tried square breathing, something my doctor taught me. I inhaled while slowly counting to four, held my breath for another four-count, exhaled to four, and waited another four to inhale again. I did this for several minutes.

Millie noticed. "Are you okay? Can I do anything?"

I shook my head, and then relief. Either the square breathing worked or Millie's sweet voice had ended the attack. That was close.

Everyone crowded around a library window, except for Millie, who sat next to me, her hand on my forearm. "Was it an anxiety attack?"

I nodded and wiped sweat from my brow.

She leaned close. "Maybe you're a vision seeker."

"A what?"

"My ancestors believed that people who had fits were vision seekers. They thought their seizures brought prophetic visions."

"That's crazy."

"No it's not. The next time you have an attack, don't fight it. Let it come on and see what happens."

"No way." I stood shakily, and we joined the others.

Demarius looked down from the window. "We could jump."

Daemon Hall was built high, and the first floor was not

ground level. In fact, the stairs to the front door were at least six feet up, meaning there would be probably an eight-to-ten-foot jump from the window.

"It wouldn't be safe," Ian Tremblin said. "We'll exit by the front door."

Millie glanced out the window. "Yeah, the front door works for me. Lucinda?"

"Whatever. Let's go."

Hands shaking, Matt pulled off his glasses and wiped them with his shirttail. "Just get me out of here."

When Tremblin picked up the lantern, I got an idea. "Hold on." I grabbed five candles from the candelabrum, blew them out, and gave one to each person, except for Tremblin; he already had the lantern. Then I pulled matches from the two matchbooks, and tore the strips of flint into six pieces and passed them out. "Just in case."

"And the book, Wade. Bring the *Book of Daemon Hall*," Ian Tremblin said.

"Are you nuts?" Demarius blurted out. "One minute it's blank—the next, Millie's story is in it. That thing ain't right."

"We will not leave it."

"It might come in handy." I grabbed the *Book of Daemon Hall* from the pedestal and joined the others at the door leading to the hallway.

Demarius shook his head. "Crazy, both of you."

Ian Tremblin cleared his throat and gave instructions. "Matt and I will lead with the lantern. Then Demarius and Lucinda. Wade and Millie, bring up the rear."

"The buddy system," Lucinda said.

We moved into the hallway and started for the front of the house. Blackened hinges hung useless next to entries where doors had once been. Portions of the wall had burned away, leaving gaps into black rooms.

Something brushed my wrist, a calming touch; Millie, pale and frightened, took my hand. "I hope you don't mind."

I smiled at her and concentrated on the warmth of her hand. I felt her pulse, or maybe it was mine, maybe both of ours beating in sync.

"You know what this is like?" Lucinda asked.

Matt said, "I'm not in the mood for creepy analogies."

"It's like being at the beach and in water up to your neck. Someone yells 'Shark!' and you have to make it thirty or forty yards back to shore, all the while waiting for that moment of impact when the shark rips into you, its teeth—"

"Okay, okay!" Matt interrupted. "I get the picture. Thanks a lot."

"We're at the entrance hall," Ian Tremblin said, when we got to the foot of the soot-blackened marble staircase. The lantern illuminated a dozen steps before gloom claimed the rest.

Demarius gazed up. "Know how much money it'd take to get me up there?"

Lucinda raised an eyebrow. "There's not enough in the world, right?"

"Oh, I'd do it, but only Bill Gates could afford that bribe."

Peering across the massive foyer, we could just make out the entrance. The night outside dimly shone through the opening where the twin doors once stood. A portion of the ceiling had collapsed, dropping rubble to our left.

"There's something over there." Demarius pointed to the debris.

Ian Tremblin held out his lantern and stepped slowly toward a monster that sat crookedly on the floor. "A gargoyle." The car-sized statue was a combination of man and reptile with wings and horns. "It must have fallen from the roof during the fire."

"Let's get out of this dump." Matt's voice was flat in the cavernous room.

Eyeing the gargoyle, Lucinda said, "I'm with Scungilli."

Our buddy system coalesced into a small mob as we carefully crossed the entrance hall. It seemed to take forever, but we finally stood before the gaping entrance.

"Go on, Mr. Tremblin," Demarius said impatiently. "Let's get out."

"Almost seems too easy." He stepped over the threshold, but no one followed.

I was at the back of the pack and pushed through them. "What's the holdup?"

Tremblin stood on the other side of the door, his back to

us—and somehow, impossibly, he stood before a dark hallway. I blinked hard. He should have been at the veranda steps leading down to the long-dead lawn, but there was no veranda, there was no lawn—everything outside the doorway was replaced by a murky corridor. Goose bumps flared on my body as I recognized where he was. I looked across the entrance hall and up the great staircase to where a solo figure stood, barely illuminated by the lantern he carried. I looked back out the front door and saw the same man.

Matt murmured a chant: "It's not possible, it's not possible, it's not possible."

Mired in numbness, I stumbled through the doorway and stood next to Tremblin. It wasn't an optical illusion. I had stepped out the front door and onto the second floor.

Ian Tremblin shook his head in anticipation of my question. "I don't know, Wade. This defies every physical law of space. Einstein himself couldn't explain it."

The others passed through the door, and we stared into the torched hallway ruins. Mr. Tremblin's lantern shed enough light to see a missing section of floor that started just within the borders of our illumination.

Lucinda started to say something but only produced a dry gasp. She swallowed and tried again. "Now what?"

I turned and stared out at the great entrance hall from the second-floor landing.

"This is insane," Matt muttered, and dropped to his knees.

Demarius looked at me, his face a sickly pallor. I wanted to say something but could only stare back. Matt screamed, making me jump. He pushed up from the floor and ran down the hallway toward the hole in the damaged floor.

"Wait!" I dove for him and brought him down hard. He fought, kicking and scratching, trying to get away.

Millie knelt by his side. "Matt, calm down, calm down." She spoke soothingly and put her hands on his cheeks. "Shhhhh. It's all right, shhhhhhh."

He stopped struggling, but wept loudly. I climbed off him.

Lucinda knelt on his other side. "Hey, Scungilli, we'll look out for you."

"Scary," I muttered.

"A regular frightfest," Lucinda added, wide-eyed.

"I'm going to need a change of underwear," Demarius said.

Matt's face was smudged with ash. Clean, vertical lines on his cheeks marked where his tears had passed, and unexpectedly, he laughed.

"Oh, yeah." Lucinda stood and brushed her hands on her thighs. "A little bathroom humor cheers him right up."

"It's a guy thing," Demarius said.

Matt got to his feet with a self-conscious smile.

Ian Tremblin strode to the staircase and gazed down as far as the limited light allowed. "Mr. Matthews, do not be embarrassed. All of us are frightened. But you need to let your impressive intellect override your emotions." He turned to the young contestant. "We need your help if we're to get out."

I patted Matt on the shoulder and gave him a weak smile. He pulled the glasses from his nose and wiped at his face.

Ian Tremblin walked a little into the hallway and lowered the lantern. "You're lucky that Wade stopped you." He gestured to the portion of floor that had collapsed in the fire. "The upper floors of Daemon Hall are dangerous."

"Should we try the front door again?" Lucinda asked. "Or a different door out?"

"I fear that no matter how many doors we step through, the result will be the same—we'll find ourselves right back here."

I agreed. "Daemon Hall wants us on the second floor."

"Then we go back to my plan and jump from a window," Demarius said.

"We're on the second floor now," the writer pointed out. "Factoring in the first-floor windows, which were eight to ten feet up, along with the incredibly high ceilings of Daemon Hall, I'd say the drop from here would be twenty, maybe twenty-five feet. We're talking broken bones or worse."

Demarius looked disheartened, then smiled. "We take off our clothes, tie them together, and use them for a rope."

Lucinda snorted a laugh.

"What? It could work."

"I was just thinking of what happens afterward. Can't you

see the headlines? 'Famous Author Discovered Wandering with Five Naked Teens.'"

Ian Tremblin rubbed his temples and mumbled, "The tabloids would love that." He looked around the second-floor landing. "We will explore Demarius's suggestion and get to a second-floor window. Then we'll decide if we can get safely down. I'll go first."

Millie spoke up. "I should lead. I'm an experienced rock climber."

"Really? Still, I couldn't forgive myself if you fell through the floor."

"Mr. Tremblin, I'm always on climbing walls. My dad and I go climb a couple of times a year in the Adirondacks and the Poconos. I know what it feels like when support starts to give. Plus, I'm lighter. I should go first."

"She's got a point," Demarius said.

Ian Tremblin passed her the lantern and swept his hand toward the dark hall.

We hugged the wall to get by the hole that Matt had nearly run into, and tiptoed along the three inches of floor that remained. We checked rooms, but floors were missing or unsound, and several were piled with rubble, so we couldn't get to the windows. At one point, Millie leapt over a three-foot fissure and peered in a door.

"This one looks good."

We jumped the crevice, though none as graceful as Millie.

For the most part the room was intact, except for a missing wall next to the remnants of a stone fireplace. Another door led to an adjoining room that was demolished.

"Hey," Demarius said, "I think this is the room we told our stories in last year."

Ian Tremblin took the lantern from Millie and examined it in the soft light. "Yes, I think so." He chuckled quietly. "Home, sweet home."

Home, sweet home? His comment chilled me.

Charred planks stood where bookcases had been. A couple of animal-head trophies remained on the wall, though they'd been burned into unrecognizable shapes. The windows had no glass. Millie, Lucinda, and I stood at one; the rest at the other. What we saw was not encouraging. We were high up, and the ground was lost in darkness.

"I'm not sure all our clothes tied together would be long enough," I said.

"Then we climb down as far as it goes and jump the rest," Demarius answered.

Millie voiced another problem. "There's nothing to tie a rope to."

"Someone could hold it while we go down," Demarius said hopefully.

"They'd have to stay, since there'd be no one to hold it for them," I pointed out.

Ian Tremblin interrupted us by clearing his throat. "I'd like to try something that's been gnawing at me since we arrived. Think back to our first contest, Wade. We were stuck here until what?"

"Until we told all the stories."

"Correct. This time we've gotten together to share a limited number of stories that coincide with titles listed in the *Book of Daemon Hall*. Perhaps, if we tell those stories, then like our previous night here, we'll be free to leave."

"That's pretty stupid reasoning." Lucinda made a face when she realized what she had said. "Sorry, Mr. Tremblin, I didn't mean you were stupid—uh. . . ."

I could see the wheels turning in Demarius's head. Yeah, what Ian Tremblin suggested would sound lame to anyone who hadn't been with us that night. But to Demarius and me, it made sense.

Ian Tremblin held out a hand. "Wade, pass me the book. The next story up in our cavalcade of terror—sorry, I sound like the crypt keeper, don't I? Matt, yours is next."

"Mine? Come on, Mr. Tremblin. Lucinda's right, it's a dumb idea. *The house wants storytime?* That sounds crazy."

Demarius lost his temper and poked Matt in the chest. "Hey! You didn't believe us in the first place, did you? Look around. We were right, you were wrong. So I think you better start listening to us and read your stupid story."

Matt looked down and mumbled, "I left my notebook downstairs. We all did."

"Hmmm." The writer pulled at his beard. "You'll have to recite it from memory."

Matt cringed. "Word for word?"

"You wrote it and know it well. Tell it as you would a story around a campfire."

"Hold on." I retrieved the *Book of Daemon Hall* and held it out to Matt. He reluctantly took it. I reached past him and flipped it open to the page headed "A Promise for Bones."

"It wrote out Millie's story, remember?" I tapped the page with a finger. "Start yours and see what happens."

He hesitated, and Lucinda urged, "Go on, Scungilli. Nothing will happen. It'll prove we're right."

He stood and cradled the book like an altar boy holding a prayer book for a priest. Matt gathered his thoughts and began. "My name is Dante, and when I was twelve, I quit—" He gazed intently at the book and groaned.

"No way," Lucinda said.

He whispered, "It's writing it a little quicker than I'm speaking. It's a few words ahead of me."

Lucinda grabbed the book and read aloud, " 'My name is Dante, and when I was twelve, I quit my job at Quisling's Spirit—' it ends there." She looked at Matt. "Is that right? Is that how your story goes?"

He numbly took the book from her and nodded.

"Proof we're right."

"Shut up, Demarius." She turned to Matt. "Well, I guess you better read it."

A PROMISE FOR BONES

My name is Dante, and when I was twelve, I quit my job at Quisling's Spirit Emporium—well, ran away is more like it. I didn't get paid for my work. Instead ol' Quisling fed me and provided a floor to sleep on. The spirits came out of a bottle, but when the customers drank too much, they'd swear they saw the ghostly kind. Smelly, dirty, and dark, Quisling's sat in a narrow alley that snaked through the French Quarter.

My father sold me to Quisling. It wasn't exactly legal, but what could a kid do? Mr. Quisling, a grim man in a stained apron, paid my father six bottles of rum and twenty dollars, good money in 1929. Every night I sat on a wooden crate at the end of the bar and Quisling would put me to work when the need arose. I fetched liquor from the storeroom, cleaned up after fights or when someone got sick; after the customers peed in buckets in a back room, I dumped them in the alley. I did most everything except tend bar.

Quisling's had lots of regulars, and some of them were downright scary. One white man was captain of a tramp steamer that docked in New Orleans. His face was narrow and stubbled. He wore a soot-blackened captain's hat and rarely spoke. His eyes were faded brown surrounded by yellow, and they always seemed to be directed at me.

One old fellow told me, "Don't you ever find yourself alone with that man. He got a taste for things that ain't right."

Two people were scarier than the captain. Bones Man, they said, was over a hundred years old. Toothless, he dressed in raggedy clothes and had so many lines in his face that he looked like a prune. But no one sassed him—he was strong and had powers. Bonaparte, always in his company, was the blackest man I ever saw, and one of the tallest. Bonaparte had to take off his crooked stovepipe hat and bend his head when he came in. He wore an old black tuxedo, even on the hottest nights.

Bones Man had an intuition that told him when someone was facing troubles. He'd come in, gaze about the room until that intuition pointed out the person he was looking for.

He'd walk up to that person and say, "Bonaparte, my bones."

Bonaparte would fetch a cloth bag from a jacket pocket. Bones Man would shake the bag and dump its contents, all twenty-seven bones from a human hand. He'd read those bones and whisper in that person's ear. Their eyes might widen, or their face turn gray, and they'd nod as if accepting some terrible fate. We all hated when Bonaparte and Bones Man came in, but truth be told, they saved people from sorrow.

Once I overheard Bones Man tell a man that his wife was cheating on him; he could see it in the bones. He told that man that if he agreed to do a favor for him, well then he'd throw the bones again to see how he might fix his marital woes. It wasn't just love—he might see coming financial problems, a betrayal, even a person's death. And the worse the fate, the harder the favor; I learned that firsthand.

Things changed the night the captain paid Quisling for more than just drinks. As usual the captain sat in his corner staring at me and licking his lips with his gray slug of a tongue. At one point he went up to Quisling, ordered a drink, then leaned in close and whispered to him. I felt a shiver when they looked my way. Quisling rubbed his chin, then nodded. They shook hands, and the captain slid a pile of paper money to Quisling.

An hour later Bones Man and Bonaparte came in. The room went silent as the old man looked from person to person. His eyes locked on mine, and he strode right up to where I sat on my box. Bonaparte passed the bag to Bones Man, who knelt, shook it, and rolled the bones at my feet. He looked from them to my face, and I knew it was bad.

"What?" I managed.

Bones Man whispered in my ear. "That one bought you from Quisling." He looked over at the captain. "Tonight he's gonna take you to his ship and do hurtful things to you. When he's done, he's gonna toss your bloody corpse over the side."

I didn't even hesitate. "I'll do what you want."

Bones Man smiled. "Of course you will." He scooped the bones into his bag, shook, and dumped them again. After a few moments, he told me, "When you leave here, go left instead of right. Walk, don't run, down the alley until the problem is gone."

Not much later, Quisling told me to go home early. Home was where I slept under the kitchen table in Quisling's small apartment. I walked through the bar, past the captain, and out the door. Normally I'd go right, but Bones Man said to go left, so I did. A few seconds later, the captain came out. There ain't no lights in the alley, and each time we passed through a particularly dark patch I'd glance back and see that the captain had crept closer. I wanted to run so bad, but Bones Man told me to walk. When the captain got close, I could tell by his smile that he enjoyed this slow chase, that it whetted his appetite for things to come. He was no more than three paces behind when I passed a dark intersecting alley. A second later, I heard a grunt and turned to see Bonaparte drag the captain into it. I waited until the sounds of struggling stopped and Bones Man and Bonaparte stepped out of the shadows.

"Your problem has been remedied." Bones Man smiled. "Now, here's what you will do for me."

A year later, I was a thousand miles away working for a rich man. Now that we were into the warmer months, I enjoyed the work, though I near froze when I got there in the middle of winter. I'd never experienced cold like that in New Orleans. It wasn't like I had any choice, though. In that dark alley Bones Man told me what I had to do.

"Boy, my bones lose a little power each time I use them. For saving your young life, you have to get me a new hand from a graveyard. Collect those bones at midnight, when their powers are greatest."

"Yes sir," I said. "I'll go into St. Peter's or Lafayette and get your bones."

He shook his head and said, "Not a New Orleans boneyard. There's a special one far away, a new one on ancient ground that will provide the most potent bones."

That's how I came to work for Mr. Rudolph Daemon in the year 1930. He was building a house for himself and his family, bigger than any I'd ever seen. Mr. Daemon had a crew of over a hundred men. I was hired as a general laborer, not skilled in any one particular thing. I might help the carpenters one day, the stonemasons the next, or the plumbers. My favorite was helping Mr. McGarrity, an electrician, run wires.

"This is the kind of house a king lives in," I said one day as we took a break.

Mr. McGarrity puffed on his pipe and said, "Mr. Daemon is a king of business."

I took in the skeletal form of the massive structure. "The man must have thousands and thousands of dollars."

Mr. McGarrity chuckled. "He's worth quite a bit more. He has millions."

"Millions," I repeated, trying to get my mind around a number so big.

There was a bad feeling to that land. Most of the workers thought the site was jinxed, though Mr. McGarrity said that was just superstition. Still, they'd started building a year before the Depression, and men got injured in all kinds of accidents. Two, three, four a day were getting hurt.

"We had a lull for several weeks," Mr. McGarrity told me, "and everyone thought the run of bad luck was over. But no, that was when men started dying."

Several fell from scaffolding, two were crushed by stone brought in for the walls, and one died when his saw slipped and sliced clean through his leg.

"The man exsanguinated before the wound could be cauterized." Mr. McGarrity saw me puzzle over those words. "*Exsanguinate* means to completely bleed out. To *cauterize* is to use extreme heat to seal an open wound, even when it's a limb that's been severed."

Those were big words, words used by educated men. I'd remember them.

Mr. McGarrity paused to put a match to his pipe. "The most men died when they brought down the—

Matt stared at the book, his lips moving though he made no sound.

"S'up, Scungilli? Ghost got your tongue?" Lucinda asked.

Mouth open, he slowly moved his head from side to side. Demarius stood and checked out the page Matt had been reading, then looked at us and shrugged.

"Mr. Matthews," Ian Tremblin said, "is there a problem?"

"A problem?" Lucinda said. "I can give you a whole list."

"Shhh!" Millie directed at her.

Ian Tremblin prompted, "Matt, what is wrong?"

"The—the story. So far this has been *my* story. I mean, I don't know if it's been word for word, but"—he looked up at us—"now it's changed."

"How?" Millie asked.

We found ourselves shoulder to shoulder, circling the *Book of Daemon Hall.*

"There," Matt said, pointing to a sentence. "Remember, I took the tree out of my story? But there it is, in that sentence. See? It got back in."

Ian Tremblin adjusted his glasses. "Your work has been"—he cleared his throat—"edited."

"Who edited it?" Demarius gave voice to the question bouncing around my head.

Ian Tremblin looked into the surrounding darkness and said, "Who, indeed?"

"Well? What should I do?"

Ian Tremblin smiled uncomfortably. "Keep reading."

"Keep reading. Of course." Matt took a deep breath and continued.

"The most men died when they brought down the black tree."

One of the carpenters had a photograph of it. The tree was as black as coal, and the bark looked like scales you'd find on a snake. The trunk was as wide as a truck and twisted, and so were the branches, as if it wrestled with itself while it grew. The limbs were long, starting out thick and continuing up sixty or seventy feet, ending in sharp points. The wood had knots all over that looked like bone joints.

"Mr. Daemon wanted the entrance hall right where that tree grew. The wood was so hard it took a full day to bring it down." Mr. McGarrity dropped his voice. "Tree sap the color of clotted blood flowed where we sawed on it. That tree groaned as it fell, and that blood-clot sap sprayed everyone there."

The foreman shouted that our break was over, and as we strolled back to our work site, Mr. McGarrity continued, "A couple of weeks later, the men who had been present fell ill. At first they got achy and ran a fever. That'd last a day or two, then the fever would rage, and they'd slip into a coma."

"Coma?"

"A deep sleep no one can wake you from," he explained. "Funny thing was, the comas lasted only three days, no less, not longer. Mr. Daemon brought out doctors and nurses and set up a hospital tent. They didn't have a clue as to the affliction that struck the workmen. At first they thought things would be okay, because the sick woke up after the third day, but that was when the illness took its most dreadful turn: Their backbones went rigid and the bowing started. That's what they called it, bowing. Their rigid spine would bend backward and you could hear their bones crack. Even the toughest cried because of the pain. The fever boiled their brains at about the time their spines snapped. It was a horrible death." Mr. McGarrity shook his head at the memory.

I was nervous that it was contagious, but Mr. McGarrity said, "It only affected the men who'd been sprayed by the sap. Forty-eight out of the forty-nine men who were present died in that fashion."

"Bet that forty-ninth man feels blessed," I said.

"I do, Dante," Mr. McGarrity said, relighting his pipe. "I surely do."

"You were there, too?" Stunned, I shut up and concentrated on work until I had to ask, "What happened to the wood from that tree?"

"When everyone started getting sick, we collected it all. Well, not all of it. Mr. Daemon took some—said he wanted to make something out of it—but we burned the rest. That wood was hard to ignite, but it burned hot and made greasy black smoke."

Mr. McGarrity explained that some of the men who died had been homeless because of the Depression, and others came from away. Mr. Daemon had a small graveyard put in about a mile from the building site. Sixty-three bodies had been laid to rest before I arrived. The sixty-fourth in the ground was my friend Mr. McGarrity.

The tent hospital was long gone by the time he took sick. A doctor came out from Maplewood and looked him over. When he was done, he just shook his head.

"I thought I'd gotten a reprieve," Mr. McGarrity said, his voice weak and raspy. "I don't want to die alone. You'll sit with me, won't you, Dante?"

"I promise, Mr. McGarrity."

"I want you to have this, Dante." He put a gold pocket watch in my hands. "My father gave it to me, and his father gave it to him. I'll never be a father now, so I want to pass it on to you, from one friend to another."

For the next few days I rarely left his side. I stayed when he slipped into a coma for three days. He woke, and when the bowing was at its worst, as if he were trying to touch the ceiling with his belly, he grabbed my hand. He was so fevered it was like holding charcoal. When he died, I had to pry his fingers loose. My hand was numb all that day.

Everyone came to the funeral because Mr. McGarrity had been such a kind man. The cemetery was in a small valley, and Mr. McGarrity was laid close to the road, his grave marked with a flat-topped headstone. During the service, I decided I'd leave that very night after performing my job for Bones Man.

When most everybody was in the dining tent, I went to the toolshed, grabbed a shovel, and started for the graveyard. I stopped and went back to fetch a machete since I'd have cutting to do. It was a strange night. Even though there was a yellow full moon, it didn't provide a lick of light to see by, so it was slow going down that road to the graveyard. When I was halfway there, fog rolled in. Thick and low-lying, it chilled me from the knees down. I had a few hours to wait until midnight, so I collected wood and started a fire.

As I warmed myself, my thoughts turned to the long trip here from New Orleans. I had figured that jumping trains would be quickest, but Bones Man said not to hurry. He said I could accept rides that were offered, be it automobile or wagon, but mainly I had to get here by my own two feet. I figured that's how I'd get back once I had the bones.

"*If* you get the bones." The voice came from the direction of the graveyard.

Pinpricks of fear ran up my spine. I peered into the darkness. "Who's out there plucking thoughts from my head?"

"You know me, Dante."

And I did. I forced myself to leave the protective circle of fire-light and walked over to Mr. McGarrity. He sat on his headstone, legs crossed.

"Can't you rest, Mr. McGarrity?"

"No one rests in this graveyard." He spoke calmly, tamping on his pipe.

"Maybe when I've paid my debt to Bones Man I can move you to better ground."

Mr. McGarrity's ghost looked at me as he lit his pipe. "You're a good friend, Dante. Thank you." He exhaled phantom smoke and said, "I think it's time."

I pulled out the pocket watch he'd given me. It was closing in on midnight.

"Those buried here have no good feelings for you. They become more corrupt the longer they're in this ground. As you try to fetch a hand, they'll try to fetch you. The lonely ones are whispering that they'll drag you into their holes for company."

I shivered. "I wish I didn't have to do it, but I promised Bones Man."

"Then you're welcome to my hand. I won't harm you."

"I couldn't do that. You're my friend. You understand, don't you?"

There was no reply. He'd gone. I spoke to the still night air. "Good-bye, Mr. McGarrity."

I returned to the fire for the tools, then tromped into the middle of the graveyard and chose a grave marked by a stone cross. *This is wicked work*, I thought, and moved dirt by the spadeful. It would have been easier in New Orleans, since bodies weren't buried deep there. Because of the high water table, bodies were buried in shallow graves or placed in aboveground graves, mausoleums. But Bones Man wanted his hand from here, and I knew I'd have to dig down a full six feet. I worked steadily until I reached the coffin. After clearing dirt from the lid, I took stock of my situation. I was in a grave, and my head was belowground. I would have to climb out for the machete I'd left leaning against a headstone.

It was then I heard something move in the casket, thumping within that burial box. I jumped up and grabbed the ground above my head. I heard a squeak and looked down as the coffin lid swung open. Hanging on the side of the grave wall, I kicked my legs furiously, trying to find purchase in the crumbling dirt. The coffin's occupant sat up. Black sockets gazed up at me, and skeletal hands took hold of my ankles. It gave one tug and I fell into the coffin.

I'd seen some horrible things in my short life, but the worst by far was lying on top of that cadaver and watching the coffin lid come down. I struggled in the pitch-black box as that thing touched me all over. I screamed while it grabbed and caressed me. I fought until I heard the worst possible thing: dirt falling on the coffin lid. I gave up and lay still as the corpse stroked my face. I prayed death would be quick, and then remembered it would be a restless death in that ground. I renewed my fight, snagging something from my pocket: the chain holding Mr. McGarrity's watch. I yanked it out and the watch threw a golden glow throughout the casket. That corpse cowered under me trying to hide from it. I dropped the watch over my shoulder onto its bony face, and the cadaver crumpled into dust.

The rhythmic thump of dirt fall continued. I pushed against the lid, but its weight combined with the accumulating dirt made it hard. I shoved again, but the lid barely creaked open. I got angry and thrust up so hard that it flung wide. I stood, grabbed my watch, and saw silhouettes of corpses ringing the grave. Most were misshapen,

bent in the middle where they'd bowed before dying. They moved clumsily, stooping to grab dirt and drop it on me. I held up the watch, but it no longer shone. I stuffed it into my pocket and jumped for the side of the grave. I didn't care that the dead encircled me—I was getting out of that hole. I clutched at the ground overhead, hanging by my hands, and whimpered to see one of the dead right over me. It held the machete and slowly lifted it high.

All skulls grin—that's common knowledge—but this one had an even bigger smile as it brought the machete down in a slicing arc.

There's lots of people wandering these days, looking for work. The men who run this country, the ones who don't have to worry about food or where they'll lay their heads, say the Great Depression will be over soon. They say we should hang on and do the best we can. After going through what I did, I can tough anything out.

New Orleans didn't feel like home anymore. I returned to Quisling's, and he looked at me with shame on his face. He started to say something, maybe apologize, but he saw the look in my eyes and shut his mouth. I sat at a table and told him to bring me a drink, then paid him with a coin but didn't drink it; I simply liked ordering him around for a change. I pulled out the gold watch, it was midnight and Bones Man and Bonaparte came in. Bones Man sat across the table; Bonaparte, hat in hand, hovered behind him like a vulture.

Bones Man asked, "Did you get my item?"

I slid the cloth-wrapped hand across the table.

He picked it up, his eyes sparkling within his wrinkled lids. "From the cemetery?"

"Yes."

"Do you know whose hand it is?"

I nodded.

"Tell me, then. I am curious."

I lifted my left arm and displayed the stub of scarred flesh.

Bones Man's eyes widened. "Your hand?"

"Cut off in that graveyard."

"Who severed it?"

"The dead."

Bones Man laughed in wheezing bursts. "Tell me everything."

I didn't owe him any more, so I left Quisling's. I thought of what I didn't tell him, like how the dead returned to their graves after the corpse had sliced off my hand, and how I struggled one-handed from the grave and stumbled to the fire. I couldn't ever put into words the incredible pain of thrusting my bleeding stump into the flame, cauterizing it like Mr. McGarrity had once explained. I fainted and woke in the morning, then retrieved my hand from beside the grave. I didn't tell anyone how I got hurt. Still, Mr. Daemon was kind enough to pay for my hospital stay in Maplewood.

I saved enough money that I could've afforded train fare back to New Orleans, but I walked instead. And now that I've paid my debt to Bones Man, I'm leaving again, walking all the way back to the cemetery at Daemon Hall. I promised Mr. McGarrity I'd move his body. I keep my promises.

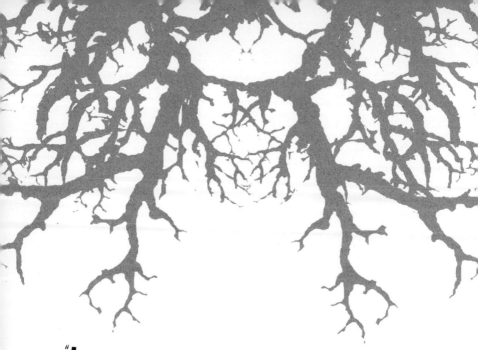

"Look!" Demarius shouted. "The sun's up. We made it through the night!"

"Morning already?" Matt gazed around wide-eyed. "Did my story take that long?"

"Wow!" I laughed. Golden sunlight came through the windows, reflecting off glass and lighting the room. Hold it. Glass? And the room—it was filled with furniture.

The *Book of Daemon Hall* fell from Matt's grasp onto a brightly colored oval rug.

Books filled newly made bookcases. A polished mahogany desk stood before the fresh bricked fireplace. Sitting on the desktop were a lamp and writing implements. Plush green curtains hung at the sides of the windows, while paintings of foxhounds and men on horses hung on the wall, above which were perched animal-head trophies.

"When did this . . ." Lucinda's voice faded.

"Amazing," Ian Tremblin said.

Demarius ran to the adjoining room, and I rushed to the hallway door.

"The bedroom is all new," he called.

The hall was full of light, and for a brief second something flickered and flew past at incredible speed. It was no more substantial than a shadow seen out of the corner of my eye. I swallowed, then turned back to the room. "Everything is new out here, too."

"This means we can leave, right?" Lucinda grinned.

Relief flooded through me.

"Wait." Ian Tremblin's face turned ashen. "Something's not right."

"What do you mean?" Demarius asked, laughing. "It's morning. We can walk out, just like we did when the sun came up last year."

"Demarius, look around." Anxiety showed on Millie's face. "Everything is new." She whirled to face Ian Tremblin. "What year would that make it?"

I didn't know what Millie was getting at, but the question stunned the writer. He grabbed at the desk, stumbled around it, and fell into the chair. Staring unfocused at the desktop, he said, "If we leave now, we run the risk of never returning home."

"Why?" Lucinda demanded.

His gaze found its way to her face. "Because it's 1933."

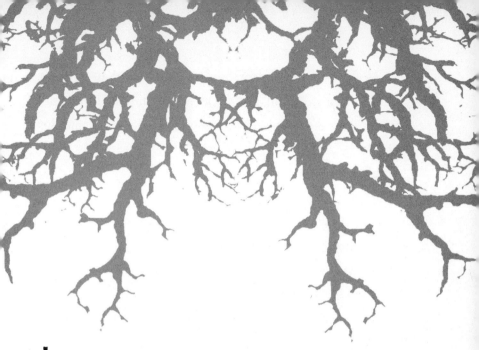

Ian Tremblin, at the desk, head in his hands, mumbled, "I need a moment to think."

We went into the adjoining bedroom.

"Impossible," Matt repeated for the umpteenth time.

My stomach was all twisted. I pulled aside the drape by the window and peered out. "They finished building Daemon Hall in 1933. Look, over there. That's where they've stacked the construction scaffolding."

Matt took another firm step into denial. "There's no way."

"Notice anything unusual?" Demarius asked. Lucinda started to make a sarcastic remark, but he cut her off with a glance. "It's hard to see, but things are moving."

It was subtle, but I saw it. Everything stayed in place, yet kept shifting.

I decided to bring up something that concerned me. "I don't want to freak anyone out, but be careful around Mr. Tremblin." I looked to the door, making sure he hadn't followed us into the room.

"Why?" Millie asked.

How could I explain this?

"I'm just saying we can't completely trust him."

"Why not?" Lucinda sounded put off.

"Last year Daemon Hall kind of possessed him. What if that connection is still there?"

"What are we supposed to do? Run off? Abandon him?" Matt asked.

"No. At least not yet. All I'm saying is keep an eye out for strange behavior."

Lucinda snorted. "That'll be hard. He's a strange man."

Millie looked thoughtful. "Have you noticed anything in particular?"

"Remember how he laughed when he realized we were in Daemon Hall?"

"People react to scary surprises in different ways, including the giggles, but if you're worried, then we'll keep an eye on him." Millie looked back out the window. "Wait a minute, it's not things that are moving. It's the shadows moving around the objects casting them. See? They're getting longer, too."

"I better go tell Mr. Tremblin," I said.

He was still at the desk and looked up when I came in. "All that we see or seem is but a dream within a dream."

"What?"

"Quoting Edgar Allan Poe's 'Dream Within a Dream.' My way of saying that things aren't always what they appear to be in Daemon Hall, are they?"

"No sir."

"I'm planning a book on scientists who take a methodical approach to ghost hunting. So, I've developed a haunting grading system, something based on the Close Encounters UFO rankings."

"Like in *Close Encounters of the Third Kind*?"

"The scientist in the movie was based on Dr. J. Allen Hynek, an astronomer who conducted UFO investigations for the air force. The list has grown, but initially he devised three rankings. The Close Encounter of the First Kind is a visual sighting. The second is physical evidence. The third indicates sightings of aliens in or around the craft."

"How would you do that with ghosts?"

"A first-stage haunting would be strange occurrences: oddities caught on camera, electronic voice phenomena, electromagnetic spikes, that kind of thing. A second-stage haunting means ghosts are seen. They interact with the living for the third stage. A fourth-stage haunting would denote malevolent ghosts who intimidate or harm people."

"Daemon Hall is a definite fourth-stager."

He gave a weak chuckle and nodded.

"Mr. Tremblin!" Demarius ran in, trailed by the others. "It's almost night already!"

The room darkened as if someone was lowering blinds over the windows.

"I know, I was just about to show Wade." He gestured to the fireplace. An old-fashioned clock sat on the mantel. The minute hand lapped faster than a spinner on a board game. The second hand spun so fast it was invisible. The hour hand marched through each rotation in a matter of seconds. "Time is passing at phenomenal speed, yet it's not constant. The first hour I timed flew by in less than ten seconds. The next lumbered by at a leisurely forty-eight seconds, and this most recent hour took twenty seconds to complete."

"You're losing me," I said. "An hour is—well—an hour."

"Yet it is night already." Tremblin relit the lantern. "Mr. Matthews, I assume you read science fiction."

"My favorite kind of book."

"With your intellect, I would dearly love your take on what is happening."

"Whoa!" I blurted out as a man took shape at one of the windows. He didn't walk in; he was just there, at the window, with his hands clasped behind his back. The next second, he vanished. "Tell me you guys saw that."

Lucinda rubbed her eyes. "Who do you think it was?"

"Did you notice his clothes?" Millie grabbed my arm. "They were old-fashioned."

"I think I understand." Matt pushed his glasses into place and excitedly said, "Time is passing at its normal pace; we're the ones out of the norm. Somehow we have been pushed out of the time stream."

"Hold it, hold it. I read science fiction, too," Demarius said. "You're saying that we not only got knocked *back* in time, but *out* of time as well?"

"I'm not following," I admitted.

Ian Tremblin explained. "They're discussing the time stream continuum. Think of time as a road: Everything on it moves ahead at the same pace. If you get off the road and move either forward or backward, then get back on the road, that would be time travel."

"Keeping with that analogy"—Matt's voice took on his computer-nerd-it-all tone—"we have gotten off, traveled back, and somehow ended up on a poorly constructed alternate route. For us, time passes at different speeds."

Ian Tremblin nodded. "One of the first books to broach this subject is the classic *The Time Stream* by John Taine, though the book won't be out for another dozen years."

"Huh?" Demarius grunted.

"Published in the mid-forties—we're in the thirties."

Matt nodded. "I was thinking more along the lines of Michael Moorcock's time stream series, but yes, the same idea."

"Hold on there, Scungilli," Lucinda interrupted. "If that guy whizzes around faster than a hummingbird, then we must be moving like molasses."

I knew what Lucinda was getting at. "They'd see us. We'd look like statues."

"Mmmmm," Matt mused. "Maybe this alternate, intermittent time stream acts as a one-way mirror. We can see them, but not the other way around."

Ian Tremblin cleared his throat. "I, too, have a theory. There's a type of haunting called *residual*, or, the term I prefer, *cinema of time*. Sometimes ghostly events occur exactly the same each time they're witnessed. People who venture to the battlegrounds at Gettysburg at night often see Civil War battles. Some paranormal investigators believe that events, due to strong emotional energy, can imprint themselves on the environment and then repeat over and over like a supernatural video. This could be similar, such as Daemon Hall showing its memories. If it's only recollections of the past, what would happen if we left? Would we walk out the door and find that we're in our proper time?"

"But"—Matt held up a finger—"if this is time travel, we'd be in 1933. We'd be dead from old age by the time we got to the year we were born."

"That's nuts, Scungilli," Lucinda said.

"I can prove it. That man we saw probably stood at the window for five or ten minutes, his time of course. He was immobile long enough that we could see him, even if for just an instant.

It's night, so the Daemons will be sleeping and lying in one spot long enough to be visible. If we can see them, that proves we're outside the time stream looking in."

"Or it means Daemon Hall is replaying its memories of the Daemons asleep."

They flailed around with theories, and I was losing patience. "Look, judging from what went on before and what Mr. Tremblin, Demarius, and I learned from it, the answer lies *inside* this mansion, not what year it is outside. Our survival depends on us—in here."

"Let me guess," Lucinda said. "Our stories?"

"Do you have a better idea?" I snapped. "Seriously. After each story tonight, there have been—well—dramatic shifts in reality."

"Wade's right," Demarius said. "I mean, no one wants to get out of here more than me, but if we don't go about it the right way, well, bad stuff happens."

"It's too risky to walk out, and where would we go? Another story may provide answers," the writer said.

"Or more questions," Lucinda mumbled, and walked to where Matt had dropped the *Book of Daemon Hall*. She turned pages so roughly I thought she might rip one out. "Here. Next one is 'The Go-To Guy.'"

Demarius's shoulders sagged, and he took the book from her. "That's mine."

Ian Tremblin looked at Demarius, narrowing his eyes.

"The others said their stories came simply. How difficult was yours?"

"It was like you guys said, the easiest I've ever written. Why? Is that important?"

Ian Tremblin nodded. "It goes along with a theory that I'm developing."

"At least we have chairs to sit in," Lucinda grumbled, and dropped into one.

Demarius stared at the page and waited. "Nothing's happening."

"Start the story," Matt said. "The words will come after that, and you read along."

" 'The Go-To Guy,' by me, Demarius Keating."

THE GO-TO GUY

The doorbell rings and sweat breaks on my brow. It sounds again and I put a hand to the wall to keep my balance.

"Jimmy!" Mom yells from the kitchen. "Will you get that? It's probably Doris."

I exhale in relief and go let Mrs. Parker in. We have a brief conversation about how I'm fine and school is good, both of which are untrue. She goes to the kitchen while I stand by the door and wonder how long it will take me to get over what happened that night. It's funny the little things, like doorbells, that bring back bits and pieces: Shelley, the violence, an ice pick at my eye. I shake my head to clear those thoughts as Mom and Mrs. Parker come into the foyer.

"Jimmy, honey, Doris and I are going to the beauty parlor for about an hour. Will you be all right?" Mom asks.

"Sure," I say. "I'm fine."

"The number is by the phone if you need me. Or call your father at the office."

After they leave, I go and sit in one of the lounge chairs out back. I hope the morning sun will keep the memories at bay. It doesn't.

"Craziest release of 1967, 'The Eggplant That Ate Chicago' by Dr. West's Medicine Show and Junk Band. Welcome to the asylum. I'm Larry the Loon, and you're tuned to Crazy Radio!" A recorded chorus sang, "Rock and roll on your radio!"

Staying up late to do homework is a bummer, but Larry the Loon on Crazy Radio for the tricities made it a lot more tolerable.

"Hey, hey, you're talking to Larry the Loon on the Crazy Radio funny phone!"

"I think your radio station is terrible," a woman said. "Making fun of people with serious mental problems is just awful."

"Wow, man. That's really heavy. I never thought about it like that," Larry said, in a rare show of seriousness.

"Well, you should, especially with Morningside Hospital for the Criminally Insane right outside of Maplewood," the woman said.

I gasped at the mention of the mental hospital I'd been in.

Demarius looked up, mouth agape. "Wade, I'm sorry. I didn't write that, but it's like that in here." He lifted the *Book of Daemon Hall*. "I wrote about Three Rivers Hospital for the

Criminally Insane. And the town wasn't Maplewood; it was a fictional place called Ashton."

Not wanting to sound like a wimp, I said, "It's all right. The book changed those things, edited your story. Besides, Morningside isn't for the criminally insane."

Demarius looked sheepish. "It used to be. I did some research. Morningside was where the state housed criminally insane patients. They made the switch to a conventional mental hospital in the eighties."

"Oh."

Demarius looked at Ian Tremblin. "Should I keep going?"

"Wade?" the writer asked.

"Huh? Yeah, sure."

"Shoot. Where was I?"

"The phone call to the radio station," Millie said.

Demarius found his place on the page and cleared his throat.

"Well, you should, especially with Morningside Hospital for the Criminally Insane right outside of Maplewood," the woman said.

"Making all those jokes about asylums and insanity, I must be . . . must be . . . CRAZY!" Larry the Loon ended the call with his loony laugh. "Hey, some of you are putting your nose to the homework grindstone for that sanatorium known as school. But as your head lunatic at Crazy Radio, I order you to put down your pencil and crank up the volume for the Rolling Stones, 'Jumpin' Jack Flash,' brand new on Crazy Radio!"

"Thanks, Larry," I mumbled, and leaned back, ignoring my books. Crazy Radio was the coolest station. McMurphy and Nurse Ratched did some far-out stuff in the mornings. Lizzie Borden ran the midday show, complete with ax-whack sound effects. Trustee Pete and Crazy Aunt Mabel cranked the tunes till seven, when Larry the Loon took the mike. Paranoid Paul came on at midnight, but to be honest, he made me nervous.

It's a gas gas gas! Mick Jagger brought the song to a close, and Larry came on, "Hey, inmates! In twenty minutes I'll give away a groovy prize—Winner's Choice Saturday! Hang out for your chance to win on Crazy Radio!"

I looked at my homework. What a drag. I slammed the book shut and stuffed my half-finished report into a drawer. It was Thursday night. My mom and the old man were going away for the weekend, leaving the next morning. I decided not to crack another book until the weekend was officially over.

I threw on a pair of sweats and lay on my bed. "Fire" by the Crazy World of Arthur Brown came on, and I stared at the ceiling, thinking about the weekend. It would blow my mind to get Shelley DeCamp over. "Hey, Shelley," I'd say, "come to my pad for a little free love." She's such a turn-on. Tall, long black hair, those beautiful eyes. But reality can be a drag; Shelley hardly even acknowledged my existence.

"Hey, inmates! Time for the contest. We'll supply whatever the winner wants for Saturday night, courtesy of our Go-To Guy!" Occasionally they'd talk about the Go-To Guy. He wasn't a disc jockey, so I figured he was a producer or something like that. "Caller ten will get a crazy question. A correct answer wins! It's Winner's Choice Saturday at 555-CRZY!"

I picked up the phone and dialed. I couldn't believe it when it rang. I'd always gotten a busy signal when calling for their other contests.

"Hey, hey! You're on the funny phone with Larry the Loon!"

"Really?"

"Would I lie to you, man? You're caller ten! Who is this?"

"Jimmy Stevens."

"Jimmy, I have a crazy question for you about crazy killers. In the psycho story 'The Hook,' the maniac escapes from an asylum and seeks victims on Lovers' Lane. What does he leave dangling from the door handle of the young couple's car?"

"Ummm—his hook hand?"

"Jimmy, you are absolutely, one hundred percent CORRECT!"

The doorbell rang at six on Saturday. I ran down the stairs in a new pair of hip-hugging bell-bottoms. I also wore a purple paisley shirt and a pair of ankle-high black boots. I wondered what they'd wear. I'd always had a mental image of Larry the Loon as a tall, muscular guy who dressed mod. The Go-To Guy was a complete mystery. When I opened the door, I was greeted by a lumpy toad next to a thrift-shop private eye.

"Hey, hey, Jimmy!" the lumpy one bellowed. He was short and round. Tangled red hair shot in all directions. Though he was at least thirty, acne covered both cheeks. He wore a tie-dyed T-shirt with the Crazy Radio logo emblazoned across the chest. "I'm Larry the Loon, and this is my associate, the Go-To Guy!"

It was hard to pinpoint the Go-To Guy's age. He could've been anywhere from twenty-five to forty-five. A brown fedora sat on his head, and his shoulder-length brown hair was meticulously combed. A black cigar was clamped in his mouth, the smoke thick and pungent. He wore a plaid sport coat. Underneath was a white shirt and red bow tie. Something about his eyes clued me in to the fact that he was a serious man.

The Go-To Guy took the cigar from his mouth, and softly said, "Hiya, chief."

"Uh, hi."

"Now, Jimmy, I know it's a Winner's Choice Saturday, but we have some ideas for tonight." Even in person, Larry had a deep, smooth voice.

"Yeah, well, I was just going to hang out with you," I said.

"Right on! How about dinner at Mad Hatter's?" Larry articulated. "Then you can bring a date to see Sam the Sham and the Pharaohs at the Rock House in Maplewood!"

"Wow, that'd be great, but I don't have a date, and don't I have to be eighteen to get into the Rock House?"

"Tonight you're cruising with us! Anything is possible!"

I had hoped that we'd ride around in a cool radio van, but the Go-To Guy got behind the wheel of an old junker that left a trail of

smoke as we drove across town. We pulled into the restaurant parking lot, a line of red taillights in front of us.

"Wow!" Larry said. "Mad Hatter's is busy tonight!" Larry talked in real life like he did on the radio. Everything ended in an exclamation point.

The Go-To Guy cut off an approaching car to grab a parking space. He ignored the angry honk and pulled his daisy-shaped keychain from the ignition. The old Rambler chugged, coughed, and died. Crossing the parking lot, I saw a 1947 cherry-red Chevy Fleetline in mint condition. I looked in the window at the leather seats, huge dashboard, and wood steering wheel. There was enough room to throw a party.

"This is the kind of car we should be cruising in," I said, cupping my eyes and pressing my face to the glass.

"Hey, kid!" someone yelled. "Get offa my car!" I turned and saw a guy leaning off Mad Hatter's porch railing. He wore a cowboy shirt and had a beer belly the size of a beach ball. "Put your damn hands on my car again, and we're gonna have problems."

"Yeah, sure," I said. "Sorry."

The man turned to someone and said, "Can you believe that stupid kid?"

Embarrassed, I looked at Larry, and he shrugged.

The Go-To Guy, however, stared at the man and chewed on his cigar. Then he started for the restaurant, and we followed. Larry and I waited by the door as the Go-To Guy went in. There were twenty-five or so people ahead of us.

"A long wait," I said.

"I doubt that!" Larry said, happily.

After a few minutes, the Go-To Guy appeared at the door and waved us in. We followed him to a woman in her mid-twenties. Blond and in a miniskirt, her eyes brimmed with tears. She led us to a booth, placed menus on the table with trembling hands, and hurried away.

"What's up with her?" I asked, nodding at her back. "She looked scared."

"Must be a bad trip," the Go-To Guy said.

Larry's loony laugh was cool on the radio, but in public, it was embarrassing.

"How'd you get a table so quick?" I asked the Go-To Guy.

He winked and blew smoke at me. "I asked her name, then told her I would get her address and pay her a late-night visit if she didn't seat us right away."

"Huh?"

"We've learned it's best," Larry said in perfect radio vocalese, "not to question how the Go-To Guy gets things done!"

Dinner should've been great; Mad Hatter's makes great burgers. Larry, though, was a bummer. During dinner he quizzed me in his dominating voice, finally turning to girls.

"So who's the lucky lady you'll bring to the concert to-night?"

"Uh, well, I don't have anyone to bring—just us, I guess."

The Go-To Guy pulled concert tickets from his pocket. "I have four tickets. It's a magic night, chief. There's gotta be somebody you'd want to go with."

"Shelley DeCamp." Her name fell from my mouth before I realized I'd spoken. "But—uh—there's no way she'd go out with me. She's popular, you know?"

"Shelley DeCamp?" the Go-To Guy repeated. "Be right back," he murmured, and slid from the booth. "Where can I find a phone?" he asked a passing waitress.

The Go-To Guy returned ten minutes later as Larry and I finished our meals.

"I'll take care of dinner." Larry grabbed the check and made for the front.

"I think I'll hit the bathroom," I told the Go-To Guy.

"And I'll take care of our transportation," he whispered.

When I came out of the restroom, I saw Larry by the cashier. The Chevy guy who'd yelled at me walked out the door. I joined Larry, and we waited for the Go-To Guy. After a couple of minutes, the Go-To Guy popped his head inside the front door and waved at us. I wondered why we were waiting for him if he was already outside.

"Hey, Jimmy! Where are you going?" I was midway across the parking lot, but they had stopped next to the cherry-red Chevy. "Your wish is our command!" Larry announced. "Here's our ride for the rest of your Winner's Choice Saturday!"

"Really?"

"Yeah," the Go-To Guy said. "Turns out the owner is a Crazy Radio fan and donated it for the night."

That was cool, I thought, and climbed in. The Go-To Guy turned the key, and the engine roared to life. I heard a couple of thumps from the back of the car.

"I need to take care of something," the Go-To Guy said and, letting the loud engine idle, he got out, went around the back of the car, and opened the trunk. After a moment he returned and we drove off.

We headed in the opposite direction from the Rock House in Maplewood, but I didn't say anything. We ended up downtown and pulled into the parking lot of the Royal Theater, where *2001: A Space Odyssey* was showing. The Go-To Guy got out.

"I'll be right back," he said softly.

Five minutes later, he exited the theater. My heart stopped when I saw Shelley DeCamp and Brian Silva with him. Oh, no! Brian would cream me good for interrupting their date. *Don't come over here, don't come over here,* I chanted under my breath. I sighed a thank-you when Brian pointed further into the parking lot and they started in that direction, Shelley first, then Brian, then the Go-To Guy.

"So, that's your beloved Shelley."

I jumped at Larry's basso voice. "How'd he find her? What's he doing?"

"Getting your date," Larry said with a smile. "Guess he called her house from Mad Hatter's and found out she was here."

"But Brian Silva is her date."

"The Go-To Guy can be persuasive."

They stopped by a sedan in the dimly lit parking lot. Someone opened the trunk. A moment later, the Go-To Guy closed it.
He pointed our way. Shelley shook her head and backed up. He
grabbed her arm, pulled her close, and spoke to her for a minute.
Had he put Brian in the trunk? Then, still holding her arm, the Go-
To Guy started back, pulling her along. I sat in shock as the door
opened and Shelley slid beside me.

"Hi, Jimmy," she said. For a second her face was tense, then
she smiled.

The smell of her perfume cut through the cigar smoke and
made me dizzy and giddy. I giggled and slapped a hand over my
mouth.

"So we're going to a concert?" Her words came to me fine, but
her lips moved in slow motion. Just watching her speak was erotic.

"Wh—what about Brian?" I stuttered.

"Um—it's you I—uh, want to be with." Then she did it. She
leaned over and our lips touched. It was better than I'd ever imagined.

The next couple of hours were mind-blowing. Shelley and I
made out the whole trip there. The doorman at the Rock House
tried to card us, but the Go-To Guy had a private word with him,
and we not only got in, but got a table up front. Larry ordered a
round of beers. I've tried beer a couple of times and have to agree
with my friend Eric Moss: it tastes like horse piss, so I just sipped
mine. Shelley, though, drank one after another. Sam the Sham and

the Pharaohs were out-of-sight. We danced for "Wooly Bully" and "Li'l Red Riding Hood." When we sat, Shelley kept a hand on my thigh.

The band finished, and Larry said, "We can stay for the late show if you want!"

The Go-To Guy looked from me to Shelley. "No. I think there's something Shelley wants to do for our winner."

She stiffened beside me. She smiled, but her eyes—I don't know—were scared? It was like she had two expressions on her face at the same time.

"I'll get some beer to go," the Go-To Guy said, and left the table.

Larry stood and stretched, then strolled up to the empty stage.

Shelley looked around the room, leaned over, and whispered, "Help me, Jimmy."

I stared at her, trying to figure out what she meant, and asked, "Help you how?"

"Shhhh," she hissed.

"Help you with what, Shelley?" Larry boomed from just behind us.

Shelley jumped at his voice. "Nothing," she blurted out. "I didn't say anything." Her mouth screwed up, and tears welled in her eyes. She looked past me and gasped, then she forced a smile. I turned as the Go-To Guy approached with a six-pack in his hand.

No one spoke as we rode around. "Spooky," by the Classics IV, came on Crazy Radio. Shelley sat at the other end of the seat. Why was she so distant now? I sensed her looking at me, and when I turned, she flung herself into my arms.

"Wha—?"

"Now!" she said. "Do it now!"

"Do what?"

She kissed me, long wet kisses with those wonderful Shelley lips. She began to unbutton my shirt. Her hand trembled, and I grabbed it.

"What are you doing?"

"Let's do it," she demanded, her teeth bared.

"Make love, not war." Larry laughed from up front.

"But—but—they're right there," I stammered.

"Let me get this over with!" Tears started down her cheeks.

"Shelley," the Go-To Guy said quietly.

"Please"—she was close to hysterics—"so I can get back and see if Brian is all right!"

"Shelley." The Go-To Guy drew out her name so softly it was almost inaudible.

"Oh, God, I can't do this!" Shelley leaned away and sobbed.

"The date is over." The Go-To Guy spun the steering wheel to the left, cutting across two lanes, the wheels squealing. He nearly sideswiped one car and came close to clipping another. Blaring horns diminished as he accelerated.

"Wait!" Shelley pushed even closer to me. "I'm okay. I just had too much beer."

"The date is over," the Go-To Guy repeated, and hit the brakes.

We skidded to a stop just past a Ford sedan in the movie theater parking lot.

"I'll do what you want. I'm smiling, see, just like you said." Shelley's mouth stretched into a toothy grimace.

The Go-To Guy leapt from the car, snatched open the back door, and before I knew it, Shelley was gone.

I jumped out. "What are you doing?"

The Go-To Guy shoved me and I fell, hitting the back of my head on the car door. Through swirling starbursts, I saw them by the Ford. He gripped her wrist, and she fought to get free. Then she stared at me, silently pleading. Black mist filled my vision. I shook my head until I could see again. The Go-To Guy stood alone before the Ford's open trunk, his back to me. He slammed the trunk shut.

Still dazed, I got to my feet. "Where's Shelley?"

The Go-To Guy pushed me into the backseat, got behind the wheel, relit his cigar, and we drove off.

There was a burst of light like someone had taken a flash photo. It came again, over and over.

"Mr. Tremblin?" Millie asked.

"My goodness, it's the time," he responded.

Time flow was going so quickly that night and day passed in mere moments. It was like someone stood by the light switch flicking it off and on.

"Check out the clock," I said. The hands were spinning so fast they looked invisible.

"Maybe it's good," Demarius said. "Maybe we're getting to our time faster."

Ian Tremblin looked cautiously around, then said, "Continue."

Resting my head against the window, I tried to make sense of what had happened. Streetlights and oncoming headlights played over the interior of the car. I wished that I could go home but was scared of what they'd do if I asked.

After a while Larry the Loon said, "Hey, Jimmy! There're the Crazy Radio studios."

I didn't respond.

"It's right over there, to the right!"

I lifted my gaze. We were out in the country, and the only building I saw was Morningside Hospital for the Criminally Insane. "Where?"

"There." Larry pointed to the asylum.

"That's Morningside."

"I know! We live there! We work there, too!"

"Huh?"

"Crazy Radio is part of a treatment program—you know, the responsibility of holding a real job. Sure, we call ourselves *Crazy Radio*, but most people think that's because we're crazy, wild party people. I don't think our audience would be too thrilled to know the station was literally run by criminal lunatics. We like to keep that quiet. All our giveaways are usually records, gift certificates, and concert tickets, things we mail to our winners! Some of us thought it would be a gas if we could actually interact with our listeners for a change. And you're that lucky listener, Jimmy! Trustee Pete has access to keys and helped us get out."

Have you ever sucked on a milk shake and gotten brain freeze? Only this was a simultaneous brain freeze, stomach freeze, and groin freeze. They *were* crazy, criminally insane! Some of what had happened started to make sense. The car we'd driven around in all night—the Go-To Guy had taken it from that loudmouth at Mad Hatter's. What had happened to him? I remembered the noise coming from the back when we first got in. What would I find if I opened the trunk? And what about the trunk of Brian's car?

"Pull over," I blurted out.

"You're the chief," the Go-To Guy said, and slowed the Chevy.

I jumped from the backseat while we were still rolling. Mad Hatter's hamburger erupted from my mouth. I stayed on my knees until I was sure I was done. Looking around, I noticed we were on one of the hilly roads north of Maplewood. In the distance, I could make out the silhouette of that creepy mansion, Daemon Hall.

"Hey, Jimmy!" My stomach lurched at the sound of Larry's voice. "What's wrong? Is Winner's Choice Saturday too groovy for you?"

The Go-To Guy leaned against the car, watching me with a crooked smile.

Larry stood over me and babbled some more. "You still have

over an hour until midnight! Over an hour left with Larry the Loon and the Go-To Guy!"

I'd had it. Pointing at Larry the Loon, I said, "Can't you shut him up?"

"You're the chief." The Go-To Guy pulled the cigar from his mouth and flicked it to the ground. He reached into his jacket and pulled out a small black pistol.

"Uh-oh, bad scene!" Larry said.

I tried to move, to speak, but I was frozen. The Go-To Guy walked up to Larry, grabbed his ear, and pulled him away from the road.

Larry's voice rose an octave. "Jimmy, come on! I thought we were pals!"

The Go-To Guy pulled Larry into some brush. There were two rapid pops and, a moment later, a crash in the undergrowth.

The Go-To Guy stepped from the scrub. "What next, chief?" he asked calmly.

I didn't answer; I couldn't. Dazedly I returned to the car and fell into the backseat.

The Go-To Guy closed the back door, climbed into the front, and drove off, humming along with "Judy in Disguise (with Glasses)" by John Fred and His Playboy Band.

Later he turned and said, "Closing in on midnight, chief. I'm gone after that. Anything else the Go-To Guy can do for you?"

"Can you make me forget tonight?" I mumbled.

"You're kidding me, right?"

"Kidding? Hell, no! I wish I could forget everything that's happened!"

The car slowed, turned right, and stopped. We were back at my house. The Go-To Guy opened my door, leaned in, and covered my face with a chemical-smelling cloth.

Before I lost consciousness I heard him say, "You got it, chief."

The fluorescent lights blinked three times and turned on, causing a sharp pain between my eyes.

"Oh, my head," I moaned.

"Don't worry, chief. The headache is just a side effect of too much chloroform."

"You drugged me?" I had trouble talking.

"Anesthetized. I put you *O-U-T*."

"Why?"

The Go-To Guy came into my limited view, lowering his face until we were only inches apart. "You told me what you wanted for your Winner's Choice Saturday."

The smell of stale cigar smoke intensified my headache. I couldn't move. I was flat on my back, arms and legs outstretched and anchored. A strap of some sort across my forehead prevented me from turning my head, so it took me a moment to realize I was in my own house, down in the basement.

"Why am I tied to Dad's pool table?"

He grinned. "So you don't hurt yourself during the operation."

"Huh?" Numbness gave way to fright.

"Come on, chief. What was the last thing you told me? You said, 'I wish I could forget everything that happened.' Right?"

"Yeah, but I was—"

He backed out of my vision. "I'm the Go-To Guy. I deliver."

"But what are you—"

"There's a treatment that the troublemakers at Morningside undergo. It's called a transorbital lobotomy."

"Lobotomy?"

"Rather have a bottle in front of me than a frontal lobotomy." He chuckled.

"Lobotomy?" I repeated.

"Transorbital, a simple procedure. They take an implement not unlike this"—he held up the ice pick from our kitchen—"and insert it between the top of the eye and the eyelid." I twisted violently back and forth. The Go-To Guy rambled on. "Then they take a mallet, I'll use this"—he held up my father's hammer—"and give the ice pick a sharp rap to get it through the skull. That's the thinnest part of the skull, behind your eyes."

"No! Nooooooo!" I pleaded.

"Then I'll wiggle it back and forth, scrambling the frontal lobe. Guess I'll have to go a bit deeper than usual to ensure you forget *everything*." He lowered the ice pick.

I screamed and there was a crashing noise upstairs followed by the sound of footsteps rushing into the basement. The police grabbed the Go-To Guy as the ice pick was a quarter inch from my right eye.

The Go-To Guy had used his gun twice before he shot Larry the Loon. Once on the Chevy guy and once on Brian. Shelley flipped out when the Go-To Guy shut her in the trunk with Brian's body. Someone heard her screaming and called the police. She told them that I was in on it, and they came to arrest me. Of course that changed when they saw me strapped to the pool table. They locked up the Go-To Guy, and everything should be okay, right?

Wrong. I can't go anywhere because most of the kids think I *did* have something to do with it. All that *pssst-pssst* whispering is a bummer. I saw Shelley a few weeks ago at the ice cream shop, and she burst into tears. The principal called my parents and said it would be a good idea to change schools.

The telephone rings, and I wait for my mom to get it but remember she's at the beauty parlor. I push up from the lounge chair and leave the warm morning sun.

"Hello."

"Hiya, chief," a whispery voice says.

What feels like the pitter pat of frozen rat paws runs all over my body.

"Good news, I got out again. And don't worry, I'll catch up to you before they find me. I'm bringing the proper surgical tools this time. The Go-To Guy won't let you down."

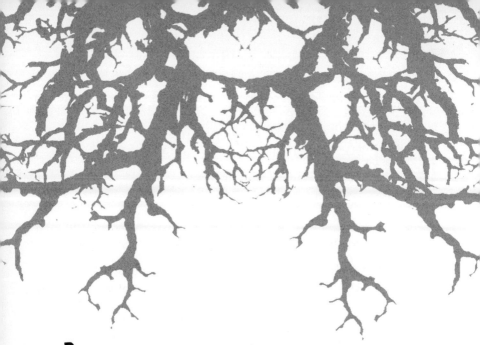

Day and night alternated over and over, which added to the creepiness of Demarius's ending.

Lucinda sat wide-eyed. "That was sick."

"Sick as in 'that's cool,' or sick as in . . . sick?"

"Both."

I took the *Book of Daemon Hall* from him and set it down. "Reminds me of an evil genie story. He grants your wish, but it has a horrible outcome."

Ian Tremblin smiled. "You not only researched Morningside for your story, but you also studied the music and lingo of the late sixties. Well done."

"Why's research a big deal?" Lucinda asked. "Especially if it's fiction?"

"When readers start a story, the author invites them to

engage in *the voluntary suspension of disbelief.* Take Demarius's story. If the characters used jargon like dude, awesome, and gnarly instead of bummer, man, and groovy, we wouldn't believe it was the sixties, and it would be harder to suspend disbelief. That's why the music had to be from that era to be convincing. An accurate factual framework firmly supports fiction."

Tremblin's impromptu writing lesson managed to distract us, but only momentarily.

Matt sat with his head down and hands stuffed between his thighs. He looked like a little kid who'd gotten into trouble. "I wish I could go home."

Lucinda snapped, "Yeah, well, I wish I had a million bucks, but that ain't going to happen either."

He looked up, his cheeks red. "Do you have to be sarcastic *all* the time?"

"Maybe I do. What of it?"

Matt's voice dropped. "I don't like you when you're like this."

Lucinda's face tensed, and I thought she was going to let loose on him, but then she sighed. "Yeah, I don't much like myself when I get like this either." She reached over and pulled him into a one-armed hug. "Sorry."

The passage of light/dark/light/dark sped up.

"Geez!" Matt blurted out, his voice muffled by Lucinda's hug.

The tempo increased until night and day oscillated at high

speed. We all stood, the strobe effect making it seem like we were moving in slow motion. In a second I was struck by intense fear, not an anxiety attack, but the deafening rumble we'd encountered when we burned the place. I remembered how we'd beat it: *Ignore it, ignore the effect it has on us, and we'll be okay.*

Demarius was talking softly to Ian Tremblin, who was huddled on the floor. Millie crouched behind a chair, tears flowing down her cheeks, and I went to her. The noise stopped, and we told them how to overcome the fear if it started again.

Demarius helped Ian Tremblin stand. Tremblin pulled a handkerchief from a pocket and wiped his face. "It's more than just a terrifying noise."

Matt tried unsuccessfully to control his shuddering voice. "What is it?"

"The sound of time slowing." He pointed to the mantel clock. The hands were turning at normal speed.

What sounded like a herd of buffalo charged down the hall. Two young boys flew by the door. A second later a teenage girl followed.

"You better run!" she bellowed.

"Cornelia?" Ian Tremblin snatched up the *Book of Daemon Hall*, rushed to the door, and peeked out after the fading footsteps. He turned to us, eyes ablaze. "Rudolph Daemon's daughter. And she was chasing Bartholomew and Thomas, her twin brothers."

Stunned, we trailed the writer into the hallway. Cornelia

shouted, and we followed her voice to the second-floor landing. We gazed down at them standing by the front door.

"I knew time was flying by, but I didn't realize how quickly," Tremblin said. "Judging from the age of the Daemon children, I'd estimate that we're now in the late thirties—no—the early forties."

Cornelia cornered her brothers at Daemon Hall's front doors. They wore matching brown shorts, white shirts, and suspenders. Their sister had on a white dress with pink stitching and wore a large red bow in her hair. "You broke my French bébé doll!"

Not wanting to be seen, we hovered on the landing several steps behind the banister. It was weird, watching what seemed like normal behavior from three kids who would die violently before they got a chance to grow up.

"Why are you running around with that?" Cornelia demanded.

The boys each held the end of a coarse rope; the length of it lay on the floor between them.

One said, "We were playing crack-the-whip—and I lost my balance—and fell against your desk—and the doll fell off—and—and—sorry."

"What's going on?" A voice boomed behind us, making me jump.

A tall, trim man stood on the landing with us. He had high, thick hair and a gray suit and tie. In one hand he held a pair of reading spectacles. In the other he held a book.

"Look," Demarius whispered. "It's the *Book of Daemon Hall*."

It was the book, but not like our version. The cover seemed new, and the title was legible. I looked from it to the copy Ian Tremblin held and back again. They were two separate books, yet the same one.

"I asked a question. What is going on?"

Ian Tremblin passed the *Book of Daemon Hall* to me. He swallowed nervously and stepped forward with an outstretched hand. "Mr. Daemon, I know you don't know us—"

Mr. Daemon? This was the man who killed his own family?

"—but let me introduce myself. My name is Ian Tremblin and I—"

The strangest thing happened then. Rudolph Daemon walked right through Mr. Tremblin and descended the stairs. The writer stood off balance a moment, then crumpled to the floor. I grabbed his arm and started to pull him up.

"A moment, just a—" he muttered. "So cold, dizzy."

"Dammmmn!" Demarius drew out the word.

"Are you okay?" Millie took his other arm.

Before Tremblin could answer, Rudolph Daemon reprimanded his children, "Haven't I told you not to run through the house? And playing tug-of-war as you go?"

"Crack-the-whip," one of the boys answered meekly.

With our help, Ian Tremblin got to his feet. He stepped forward, still shaky, and leaned against the banister to better hear what was being said.

"Where did you get that?" Daemon demanded, nudging the rope with his foot.

"We found it in our room by the door when we woke up."

The other twin pointed at his brother and laughed. "Barty thought it was a snake."

"It moved," Bartholomew explained.

"Who put it in your room?"

Bartholomew shrugged.

"And Barty said it hissed," Thomas teased.

Rudolph pointed by the door. "Place it there. I'll have the servants discard it."

Entranced, Ian Tremblin descended the stairs, the rest of us trailing behind. The writer stepped close to each of the Daemons, scrutinizing every little detail.

"Father, they broke my porcelain doll."

"Which one, Cornelia?"

"The bébé."

Rudolph shook his head. "Of course they did. It was the most expensive. Your allowances will go to your sister for a while."

"Awwww," both boys moaned.

Rudolph Daemon smiled, placed the book on the table, and knelt before his children. He took them into his arms. "We're family," he whispered forcefully. "We have to look out for one another."

"Father, something strange happened last night," Cornelia said.

"Shhh." Daemon put his finger to his lips. "Remember, we only talk about that kind of thing when we're away from the house."

One of the twins grabbed Daemon's jacket. "When are we leaving? You said we would move to a new home, one that isn't scary."

Daemon rubbed the boy's head. "We need to go together, as a family, and you know how your mother feels."

The other twin said in a pouty voice, "She likes it here."

"Well, well. The gang's all here." The voice was sultry, and we turned to see a woman enter the foyer from the right side hall. She was so stunningly beautiful my breath caught. Demarius and Matt stared with their jaws hanging. Ian Tremblin mouthed words of awe. Even Millie and Lucinda were wide-eyed at her radiance. She glided across the floor in a yellow-gold, off-the-shoulder gown. I took in her features, looking for one little flaw and finding none. Long dark hair, pale complexion, pink cheeks, dazzling blue eyes, and red lips. And her body, even clothed, was more seductive than any swimsuit model's. The *Book of Daemon Hall* slipped from my numb grasp and fell to the floor.

"Mom!" The twins ran to her and threw their arms around her hips.

She stiffened and peeled them off. "You'll wrinkle Mommy's gown."

"Narcissa, you look lovely," Rudolph said.

"Of course."

"Why don't we take a drive tonight, treat the children to ice cream."

"Nonsense. They would be up past their bedtime. Besides, several new ensembles were delivered today. I'll be too busy trying them on."

"Awww, Mother," one of the twins groaned.

"Look at the time, my little darlings." Narcissa spoke to them while stealing quick glimpses of herself in a mirror on the wall. "If you're good, I'll prepare hot chocolate." She spoke in baby talk and put a finger to each of their noses.

Lucinda growled, "If she pushed my nose like that, I'd bite her finger off."

"Oh, all right," one twin said.

"Okay," said the other.

"That's my sweet little boys. Get ready for bed, and I'll be up shortly."

They ran up the stairs like squirrels up a tree, while Cornelia stayed. "I'm thirteen. Can't I stay up later?"

"Young women need beauty rest, especially if they wish to be as beautiful as me."

Cornelia stalked off, muttering.

"Narcissa," Rudolph Daemon said, "let's discuss moving."

"Moving? But, dear, this is our home."

"Narcissa—"

"I must protest, Rudolph. I'm in too fine a mood to bicker."

She turned in a splash of twirling fabric and retreated the way she'd come.

Rudolph Daemon stared after his wife and muttered, "It's time to put an end to this." He grabbed his version of the *Book of Daemon Hall* and hurried toward the stairs.

Ian Tremblin looked at us, his face flushed. "This may be the evening he kills his family. I must follow Daemon through his bloody task, to see how he does it." While everyone was sure Daemon had committed the crimes, no one knew how. The kids were found dead in their beds, no sign of struggle, their expressions peaceful. Narcissa's body was never recovered. Daemon hanged himself from a rafter in his study—another mystery, as no one knew how he got up there with the rope. "If it's too much for you, wait here."

I picked up the *Book of Daemon Hall*, and we followed.

"He seems nice," Lucinda commented.

"Yeah," I said. "I expected a nutcase. But he seems normal."

"Yet something will send him over the edge," Ian Tremblin said.

Daemon stomped up the stairs, muttering. Bypassing the second floor, he went up to the third and traversed a couple of hallways.

Tremblin pointed out three doors. "The family bedrooms."

Daemon stopped by a medieval door in the rounded stone wall.

"It's his office," Ian Tremblin told us.

We followed Daemon in. He paced for a moment in front of his kidney-shaped desk, dropped the book on it, then went and shut the door.

Tremblin, meantime, looked at a copy of the newspaper on Daemon's desk. He tapped it. "The date is July 23, 1942. I was right. Tonight's the night."

"Hey, check this out." Lucinda stood before a glass display case set against a wall upon which several black-and-white photos hung.

Ian Tremblin glanced at the pictures. "Various stages of construction. That must be the black tree." He pointed to one photo of workmen. Behind them were the lower branches and trunk.

I peered into the glass case. "Look at this."

A plaque said "artifacts found during construction." There were buttons, pieces of pottery, a tin plate, and a sewing needle that a note card said were from an eighteenth-century village. Another card was propped on an ancient Indian bow and one arrow that said they were either from the Nanticoke or Lenape tribe. The bow was three feet long and made from dark wood. The arrow had long white feathers at one end and a chiseled black arrowhead at the other.

"How's that for a coincidence?" Demarius pointed into the case. "In Millie's story, Little Fox left her bow buried by the tree, and they actually found one."

Daemon picked up the handset of the black rotary telephone

on his desk. He stuck his finger in the dialer and spun it several times. After a moment he said, "It's Rudolph. I want it done." He listened intently then shouted, "I don't care how much it costs."

"Is he paying someone to kill them?" Matt asked.

"No, no, it has to be tomorrow morning," Daemon argued. "Meet me at the back entrance at sunrise. I want her taken from bed, out of the house, and to the hospital. She'll fight, so I give permission to use restraints." He hung up without waiting for a reply.

"He's not arranging for murder," Ian Tremblin said, amazed at the discovery. "He's trying to separate her from Daemon Hall, to have her committed."

"Then who kills the kids, hangs Rudolph"—Matt ticked off the points on his fingers—"and does away with Narcissa's body?"

Ian Tremblin looked thoughtful. "What if they never found her body because she wasn't killed? What if *she* did it and went into hiding?"

Rudolph Daemon slammed his fist onto his *Book of Daemon Hall.* "I've read this book's last damnable story! I was to record the history of my home and family in it. Instead the pages are contaminated with repugnant tales." He flung the book across the room.

"We need to find Narcissa," Tremblin said.

When Rudolph turned away, we slipped through the door.

As we reached the landing, Narcissa waltzed by the base of the staircase. Breathing hard, Ian Tremblin fell behind as we pounded down the steps. We chased after her around a corner, into the right-side hallway, and through a dining room with an incredibly long table. At the far end we pushed through a swinging door into the Daemon Hall kitchen. The room was huge, with overlarge appliances. A car-sized butcher's block was at the center. A square metal rack hung over it, from which dangled every imaginable pot, pan, and kitchen utensil. Two women in matching dresses worked at the sink, washing dishes.

Narcissa crossed the room, stopping to pick a large metal spoon from the utensils and admire her reflection on the concave side. She rehung it and moved to the women.

Ian Tremblin stumbled through the door, hand to his chest and breathing hard. "What—what—is happening?"

One of the women pointed at a steaming pot on the stovetop and spoke with some kind of European accent. "The hot chocolate is ready, madam. I'll take it right up."

"There's no need, Gretchen. I promised the children I'd bring it. You and Olivia can take the rest of the night off."

Narcissa waited until they were out of the room and retrieved a silver serving tray from a cabinet above the stove. On that she placed three large coffee mugs. Using a kitchen towel as a hot pad, she picked up the pot and poured hot chocolate into the cups.

"She doesn't look like a homicidal nutjob to me," Lucinda said.

Narcissa carried the tray to the butcher block and reached into a pocket hidden in the folds of her gown and pulled out a flat brown bottle. Smiling, she opened it and poured a few drops into each cup. She got a spoon and stirred, picked up the tray, and went through the swinging door, leaving the bottle behind.

Ian Tremblin picked it up and looked at the label. "My God, chloral hydrate."

"Which is?" Lucinda asked.

Ian Tremblin paced, staring at the bottle. "She's slipping a Mickey to her own children."

"Slipping a whattie?"

"Slipping someone a Mickey was a term used when drugging

someone in private-eye novels and movies of the forties and fifties. It was named for an actual person, Mickey Finn, a Chicago bartender in the early 1900s who would drug his clientele and rob them. She's lacing their hot chocolate with knockout drops."

"But why?" Millie asked.

"It was thought that Daemon smothered the children with a pillow, yet when they were found, their faces were peaceful. The Mickey Finn explains why they didn't struggle. But it wasn't Rudolph—it was Narcissa."

Something about that didn't make sense to me. "Maybe, but she's not strong enough to hang her husband on that rafter in his office."

Ian Tremblin rubbed his lips. "Puzzling."

"We have to stop her," Millie said.

"Stop her?" Ian Tremblin looked confused. "We can't. It's already happened."

"We have to try. Don't we?"

"But—to have the mystery solved, to see how the crimes were committed—"

"Mr. Tremblin, we're talking about their lives!"

"These are past events. There's nothing we can do."

Millie stared at the writer in disbelief. "We don't know that. We have two theories: This is either memories of past events, or we've gone back in time. If the second is the case, then we can stop it."

"Why is Daemon Hall letting us see these murders?" I asked.

"Because it wants to show how helpless we are, how we have no control here. What if we fight back and prove it wrong? We could change history."

"Perhaps," Ian Tremblin acquiesced. "How would you suggest we proceed?"

"Get a message to Mr. Daemon somehow," Demarius said.

Matt shook his head. "Have you forgotten that they can't see or hear us?"

"And we can't touch them." Ian Tremblin shivered at the memory. "It was quite painful when I came into contact with Mr. Daemon."

"Touch them?" It gave me an idea. "We've been touching things, right? We've opened doors, picked up stuff. Mr. Daemon is in his office, and what do you find in an office? Things to write with. Let's write him a note."

Ian Tremblin grinned. "I can't wait to see the expression on his face."

Matt cleared his throat. "If we can pick up things here, it voids your theory of memory while adding credence to mine that we actually made the trip back in—"

"Shut up, Matt!" Millie, Demarius, and I said at the same time.

"We'll argue the academics later," Ian Tremblin said.

We had no sooner started for the kitchen door than the sound of slowing time rumbled through the house.

"Another time burst," Matt said.

"But I didn't see day change to night or vice versa," Lucinda said.

"A brief burst," Matt answered. "An hour or two? Maybe only minutes."

"Narcissa?" It was Daemon's voice from the dining room. "Are you there?"

"Crap! He's not in his office anymore," Demarius said.

A moment later the door swung wide and the master of the house walked in.

"Quick, find something to write with," Millie ordered.

The others scrambled through the kitchen. I put the *Book of Daemon Hall* on the butcher block and searched the countertops.

After looking around the room, Daemon turned and lifted his hand to push through the door. Desperate to get his attention, I grabbed the brown bottle and threw it past his head to shatter against the wall.

Mr. Daemon went rigid and turned slowly.

"Good thinking, Wade," Ian Tremblin said, and grabbed the *Book of Daemon Hall* from the butcher block.

Mr. Daemon gazed about the room as he knelt at the broken glass. He picked up a couple of pieces held together by the label. He read it and moaned, "Narcissa, no," then rushed from the kitchen.

By the time we got to the entrance hall, Daemon was hurrying up the staircase.

"Look!" Matt nearly squeaked, and pointed toward the front doors.

The rope left by the Daemon twins was uncoiling and slithering in curly S shapes toward the stairs. As the rope rubbed against the floor, the friction produced a hiss. We backpedaled as it glided by. Dumbfounded, we watched it wind itself around the newel post and work its way up the banister. When it got to the landing it disappeared.

I knew what this meant. "Mr. Tremblin, the rope."

"The rope?" He sounded dazed.

"Mr. Daemon was hanged."

There was no reaction for a second. In the next, we raced upstairs.

"Where is it?" Demarius breathed hard as we flew around a corner on the third floor and nearly ran into—or through—Mr. Daemon. He stood in the middle of the hallway, watching as the door to Cornelia's room opened and Narcissa came out. She clutched an overstuffed white pillow.

She smiled. "Ah, you're just in time to say good-bye to the twins."

"Good night, you mean?"

"You poor, naive man. Perhaps you should go look in on Cornelia."

"Stay here!" Daemon ordered, and slid past her into their daughter's room. A moment later he wailed, "Dear God, no!" He rushed from the room, his face red. Grabbing his wife, he

154

shook her violently. She dropped the pillow and laughed. Daemon bellowed, "You poisoned your own daughter?"

"No, no, dear Rudolph, no," she spoke soothingly. "I smothered her with that pillow."

Daemon's face darkened. "Fiend!"

"No, dear, a fiend would smother them as they struggled. A loving mother would drug them so it would be an easy departure from this world." Narcissa pulled from Daemon's grasp and picked up the pillow. "Now the twins."

Daemon pushed her aside, moved to the door, and growled, "Over my dead body."

"Of course. There was never any doubt."

Movement caught my attention; it was the rope, twisting through our legs like a viper. It moved fast, the end of it rising to whip around Daemon's neck.

He grabbed at the rope but it tightened around his throat. Struggling, he begged, "Narcissa, please think about what you're doing."

She patted his cheek. "I know exactly what I'm doing. I'm fulfilling a bargain that will keep me young and lovely forever."

Mr. Daemon tugged at the rope. "What are you talking about?"

"Our house has made a promise. If I perform this one small task, I will live in these walls forever, and the mirrors will display my beauty for eternity."

"Narcissa." Tears tracked down Daemon's cheeks. "Our children—" The rope constricted, preventing any more words.

She kissed his cheek. "I'll be beautiful forever. It's worth the cost."

The free end of the rope slithered down the hallway, yanking Daemon off his feet and dragging him along. Narcissa opened the door to the twins' room and stepped in. Millie tried to follow, but the door slammed and would not open.

"Help Rudolph!" Ian Tremblin shouted.

We chased after the man whom history had wrongly branded a murderer. He gagged as his fingers clawed at the hemp, and his feet kicked against the floor and walls. His office door opened by itself, welcoming the man to his execution. I vaulted forward, trying to grab one of Mr. Daemon's legs, but my arms passed through him. My entire body jerked and shook, and I felt like I'd hugged an electrical transformer.

Demarius, Ian Tremblin, and Millie helped me to my feet. Lucinda ran past, Matt behind her. I wanted to shout at them to wait, but my mouth wouldn't work. They rushed into the office as the rope spun itself around the high beam. The last thing I saw before the door slammed shut was Matt and Lucinda watching helplessly as the rope pulled Daemon up, kicking and flailing, by his neck.

We stood at Daemon's office door. My hands stung from pounding it, trying to get in to Matt and Lucinda. I was miserable; our two friends were imprisoned within the office and we hadn't even come close to preventing the Daemon Hall murders.

"It's true, then. History does repeat itself," I croaked.

Roaring in frustration, Ian Tremblin lunged at the door. He twisted the knob, tugged, and beat on the wood. "Matt! Lucinda! Are you there?" Breathing hard, he slammed both fists against the door, then laid his head against them.

Demarius put a hand on the writer's shoulder. "We'll find them, you'll see."

He started to respond, then jerked like he'd been hit by a wave of arctic water. Demarius scrambled away as Tremblin's head flung back, mouth agape and eyes wide.

"Mr. Tremblin!" Millie reached for him.

"No!" I stopped her from touching him. She looked at me, and I shook my head. I turned to the writer. "Mr. Tremblin? What is it?"

He spun around, peering at us with dull black eyes. His lips stretched into a snarling smile. Suddenly, he yelled, "No!" and shook his head violently. He put his hands to his face and then took them away to reveal a frightened man. "Wade, hit me!"

"What?"

"HIT ME!" His face rippled, changing expression from fearful to threatening.

I swung as hard as I could, my open hand hitting his cheek with enough force to make him stagger back. When he looked at us, his eyes were filled with tears reflecting the glow from the lantern.

Breathless, he put a hand to his face. "It was trying to get into me." He sounded stunned and miserable. "Daemon Hall was trying to possess me, like last year. I think it's been trying to get me since we arrived."

"Why didn't you say anything?" I asked.

"It's been subtle: emotional changes, giddiness, anger. I hoped it was just nerves, but now, I knew it was Daemon Hall."

"How?" Millie asked.

Ian Tremblin turned away from us. "Because of the incredible rage directed toward you. For a moment I wanted to hurt all of you. You have to go on without me."

"What? We can't do that," Demarius said.

"For your own good. I'm dangerous, can't you see that? Daemon Hall could get in me at any time, and if I hurt one of you, I—" He shook his head.

I didn't like the thought of lessening our number by even one, especially if it was Ian Tremblin. He had valuable knowledge of Daemon Hall and the supernatural, and was quicker to figure things out. "Wait a minute." An idea was forming in my mind. "You don't remember anything after Daemon Hall took control of you last year, right?"

"Right," he said dismally.

"What if it works both ways? What if it doesn't know what's happening in your head unless it's in you at the time? We could come up with a secret sign—no, a secret word, a password. If we ever wonder if it's really you, we can ask you for it."

"Good idea," Demarius said. "If you don't know it, you're possessed, and we put some major distance between you and us."

"Do you think it will work?" the writer asked.

"It's better than abandoning you," Millie said.

I waved them into a football huddle and whispered, "What's the password?"

"It's gotta be something the house couldn't guess," Demarius said. "How about—"

"Shhhh! Don't say it out loud." Millie held a finger to her lips. "If Daemon Hall hears, then it won't be any good."

"Well, how are we supposed to agree on a password if we can't say it?"

I scratched my head. "We can write it out."

Demarius shook his head. "This house has eyes everywhere."

Millie leaned in even closer and spoke softly to Tremblin, "Remember the password you gave Matt so he could make changes on your Web site?"

I smiled, remembering *Afghanistan banana stand.*

"Who could forget that?" Demarius said.

"Yes, my password will do nicely."

"What if—"

Millie was interrupted by a cheerful tune with an Irish lilt.

Narcissa came humming up the hall and went into the master bedroom suite. We followed her in and across the room to her peculiar decagonal glass-shrouded dressing room that we'd been in last year. All ten walls were covered with mirrors.

Millie pointed out, "Look, none of us has a mirror image."

Narcissa, dancing as she hummed, was the only figure with a reflection. She reached to the ceiling and twirled. Her tempo increased and she spun around, until she hit a pure, high note and leapt like a ballerina through one of the mirrors. It looked as if the glass surface were made of gelatin, and she pushed through with the slightest ripple. There was only one Narcissa now, and she was inside the mirror.

"You were in there, Mr. Tremblin, last year," Demarius said.

"It gives me a bad feeling," the writer said huskily. "Let's go."

I glanced back. Swaying slightly, mirrored Narcissa hugged herself and giggled like a small girl. I fought the urge to shout curses at her and left the room.

Outside the suite, Demarius said, "Time is fast-forwarding again."

Day/night/day/night—the change wasn't fast enough for the strobe effect we'd struggled through earlier, but it was enough to keep us off balance.

"Look." Ian Tremblin shifted the *Book of Daemon Hall* from one hand to the other and pointed down the hall. Daemon's office door stood open.

We went and looked in. No body hung from the beam.

"Lucinda?" Millie called.

"Mr. Matthews?" Ian Tremblin shouted.

"Scungilli?" Demarius yelled.

A quick search of the surrounding rooms yielded no comrades. Daemon Hall was pulling a trick I was familiar with. "It's separating us."

Ian Tremblin nodded. "We must stay together at all times."

"Amen," Demarius mumbled.

Dizziness hit me—it was an anxiety attack. It started mildly, so I wasn't too concerned. The slow starters are weaker and can usually be stopped with square breathing. I went and sat in Daemon's desk chair and started counting my breaths.

"Remember what I said earlier," Millie whispered in my ear, making me jump, "about letting it come on?"

I stopped in midcount, wondering what would happen if I tried, if I sat back and let the attack roll through me. Battling was a reflexive action. Could I *not* fight it? Curious, I decided to try, figuring I could rein it in before it got out of hand. So I let it come. It was sort of like stepping outside my body, ignoring what I felt. The fit gained strength, not a lot at first, but growing, then all at once it seemed I stepped off a cliff. I couldn't breathe, and my heart beat so fast and hard it felt like my ribs might crack.

"Wade! Hey, Wade!" Demarius called.

It ended. I could breathe, and my heart eased with each beat.

"Leave him alone," Millie said, annoyed.

"But something's happening to him."

"It's all right." I opened my eyes. "A little anxiety attack. It's over."

Millie spoke softly so that the others wouldn't hear. "Did you try?"

I swallowed and nodded.

"Well?"

When the dizzying remnants of the attack passed, I said, "It was bad, really bad."

"I hate holding this thing." I clutched the *Book of Daemon Hall.* "Feels like skin."

"I'm not sure what to do," Ian Tremblin said. "Lucinda's story is next, but we have no clue where she is."

We had decided to stay in Daemon's office in case Matt and Lucinda returned. I sat in Daemon's chair and put the book on the desk so I wouldn't have to touch it. Millie was in another chair, and Demarius sat on the floor, his back against the wall. Ian Tremblin stood at one of the windows watching the hurried progression of day and night.

I could tell that Tremblin was deep in thought. He grunted, looked at me, and asked, "Was 'The Leaving' easy to write as the others professed?"

This was it, my chance to come clean, to admit I didn't have a story. No more lies, just come out and say it. Then I saw the expectation on Millie's face—I dreaded the moment it'd be replaced with disappointment. Before I knew it, I had said, "Uh, no. Not easy at all."

Ian Tremblin seemed surprised. "And no mention of Daemon Hall or Oaskagu?"

I felt like I was getting the third degree. "No. I told you that already."

"I assumed from the way things are unfolding that it would tie in with Daemon Hall. I'd hoped it would have to do with the children who vanished from the English settlement here, something along those lines."

"Sorry." Guilt was piling on guilt. I was a lousy liar.

"Would've been epic, 'The Leaving' being about the children leaving," Demarius said.

"So that's true?" Millie asked. "The English settlement and vanishing children?"

"It's history," Ian Tremblin said. "Settlers decided to take advantage of the fear the Nanticoke had for Oaskagu and built a village there in the early seventeen hundreds. There were twenty-three children, and one night all of them vanished and were never found."

"That would be an awesome story," Demarius said.

Ian Tremblin sighed. "It's a moot point now, because we're stuck. There's one story before 'The Leaving,' and that's Lucinda's, and like those children, she's vanished."

"Maybe one of us can read it," Millie said. "I mean, look what happens in the *Book of Daemon Hall* when we tell our stories."

Demarius nodded. "Yeah, we start it, the book writes it, and we can read it."

"Worth a shot," I said.

Millie came over to the desk and flipped through the pages of the book until she got to the empty page headed with "A Patchwork Quilt."

"On the other hand," I said, "we don't even know how she starts the story."

"Sure we do." Millie moved the lantern next to the book. " 'A Patchwork Quilt,' by Lucinda Taylor."

I got a sick feeling in my stomach as I watched words scratch themselves onto the page. Millie read them a second later.

A PATCHWORK QUILT

I'm a guest of the State Department of Corrections. Sucks, huh? See, Tommy, Craig, and I were bored one night and wound up behind Flite's, a tourist store that sells all kinds of beach wear, boogie boards, and sunblock by the gallon. Tommy started poking around inside a Dumpster full of cardboard boxes. We got to wondering whether cardboard burns, so we conducted an experiment. When the flames spread to the store, we panicked. Someone saw us run off, and the police found us in the park. I didn't say a thing—and I thought my boys wouldn't either. They told the cops I struck the match.

As a convicted arsonist, I'm serving a sentence at the correctional institute for juveniles. The men's prison is next to us, and though we're not housed together, only a couple of chain-link fences separate their yard from ours. I won't repeat some of the stuff they yell at us. It might make your ears fall off.

My cellmate is Warren Antonio, a born-again Christian and one-time car thief. He gave me some advice when I first arrived.

"Time comes to a standstill in here. It'll pass quicker if you get a job."

I was lying on my cot. "Can I get one in the laundry with you?"

"You can't pick a job. They put your name on a list and put you to work when something becomes available. Could be laundry, might be in the cafeteria or the library."

Sounded good to me, so I signed up and then waited for an opening.

In the cell to the right of us are a couple of goofballs, Edmunds and Rafferty—assault and burglary. The really freaky-deaky one is on our other side. Jonathan Dupree is in for murdering his girl-friend's mother.

"Hold it!" Demarius blurted out.

"That name, Jonathan Dupree, he really was a murderer," I said.

Demarius nodded. "A maniac. That was a few years ago, right in Maplewood."

Ian Tremblin's black eyes narrowed in contemplation. "And somehow he ends up in Lucinda's story."

"Another Daemon Hall connection?" Millie asked.

"I don't know," I said. "A Maplewood connection, yeah, but I

don't remember anything in the news having to do with Daemon Hall."

"Keep reading," Ian Tremblin instructed. "Perhaps the mystery will unfold."

Millie turned her attention back to the book.

It was a pretty famous case: an out-of-control daughter whose
boyfriend worships Satan and murders her protective mother. He
was only fifteen and was sentenced to life, so it was juvie prison
until he got old enough to join the hard cores. A small kid, he had
dark hair and what they call an olive complexion. Dupree didn't
have a cellmate because he'd tried to kill his last one.

There are things you instinctively know when you get locked
up. One is that it's safer in a group, so I decided I'd find one I could
hang with. At lunch one day, I approached a table of guys about
my age. They stopped talking when I sat down and stared at me
for a minute or so.

I broke the silence. "Hi. I'm—"

They turned away and got back to their conversation. In juvie
prison, we all wear short-sleeve, bright orange jumpsuits that zip
up the front. One guy, a tough Hispanic kid, was getting out in three
weeks. "Jeans, baggies—I don't care. I'll wear anything as long as
it ain't this crappy orange color. I'll even wear a dress before I do
that!"

Everyone at the table cracked up, and no one took offense that
I laughed along.

"Yeah, I know what you mean," another kid said. "Who picked this color?"

"Don't you know?" the first guy said, tugging at his jumpsuit. "They make these out of recycled traffic cones."

I laughed louder this time. It was turning into a regular chucklefest. I decided I'd cement our relationship by throwing in my own hilarious zinger. "If we ever escape, we can stand by the road whenever the cops drive by, and they'll think we *are* traffic cones."

Total silence followed. I looked from one angry stare to another.

The short-timer leaned close to me. "What are you trying to do?"

"Just juh–joking."

"Juh–joking? Don't you know the trouble you could get us in for *juh–joking* about"—he put his face right next to mine and whispered—"escape?"

"No. I mean—"

"I'm outta here soon and don't want nothing to jinx me, especially some stupid new kid. Stay away from me."

He left. They all did. As I sat there feeling stupid, I heard a totally insincere laugh behind me. I turned and saw Jonathan Dupree sitting alone at the next table.

"Traffic cones. That's funny." He had a feminine voice. "Name's Jonathan Dupree."

He held out his hand. I didn't shake it.

"Your name's Carlisle, right?"

I nodded.

"It's tough when you first get here." He leaned forward, hands clasped. "You were sucking up to those idiots because you're looking for protection, right?" He didn't wait for a response. "No one bothers me. They're scared of me. I go about my business without so much as a word from the worst of them. It could be the same for you. You don't have to be afraid of anybody."

Not being afraid sounded really good. "How?"

Dupree smiled, unzipped his jumpsuit, and pulled it open. He had a tattoo on his chest. The art was top quality, but the subject matter was bizarre. Beginning just below the neck and extending to his belly was the image of a flaming pool of water. Amid the flames was an upside-down face, as if it were Dupree's own face reflected in the pool. Though it was only black and white, the incredible job of shading provided amazing details and dimensionality. The eyes were oversized and shone with insanity. The mouth revealed serrated teeth that would make a shark envious. The tattoo face, in turn, looked like it had been tattooed. Hundreds of small figures, some kind of strange lettering, started at the forehead and went from side to side, all the way to the jaw.

"If I get a tattoo, they'll leave me alone?" I said, forcing my gaze up to his face.

"No," he chuckled. "I'm just showing you what I truly look like—my demon self." He leaned closer, staring into my eyes. "I can show you how to give yourself to Satan, and then, as your father, *He* will protect you from all harm and give you everything."

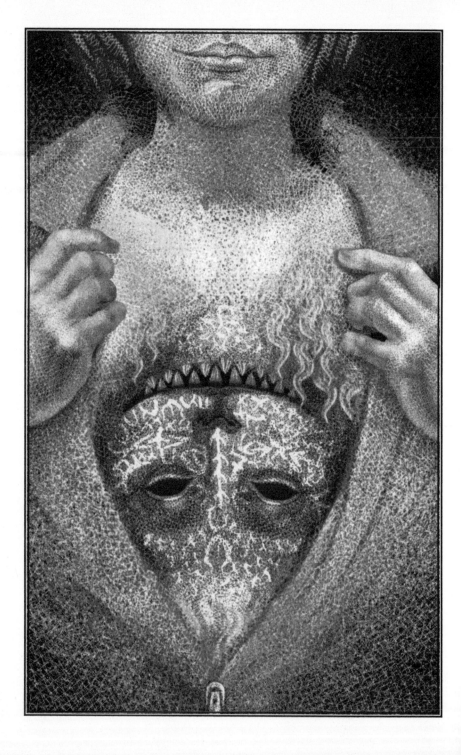

Nutcase alert! "Uh-huh." I started to stand, but he pushed me back into my seat.

"Just hear me out. As there are churches, places where religious sheep gather to seek the light of righteousness, there are places of power for those who seek darkness. I'm from Maplewood, and outside of town there's an old mansion people claim is haunted."

"Is it?" I asked.

"Oh, Daemon Hall is much more than that. I went there out of curiosity."

Millie stopped and looked at me. There it was, the Daemon Hall connection. Ian Tremblin and Demarius were as wide-eyed as I'm sure I was. As if to accentuate the newfound relationship between Lucinda's story and Daemon Hall, the thundering roll of time slowing echoed through the halls. Millie coughed quietly and read more.

"Did you find anything?"

He smiled. "It's more like something found me. A voice spoke to me. Each time I stepped into that place, it welcomed me back and told me secrets. It showed me things."

"Like what?"

"Awesome, violent, perverse things. Once the voice led me to a room of mirrors where I saw my reflection as this." Dupree rubbed his chest. "So I got my tattoo as a constant reminder. But enough about me. Do you seek protection?"

"What do I have to do for this . . . protection?"

Jonathan smiled. "Have fun, create chaos." His brow knotted, and his smile turned to a sneer. "Beat the life from those who offend *Him*."

"Kill?"

"I'm speaking specifically of that Jesus-loving cellmate of yours. We can make it look like an accident—or suicide."

"Warren's a good guy. What do you have against him?"

Dupree sneered. "He's a Christian, for one thing. And he interrupted me as I offered a sacrifice to my dark lord. You see, my cellmate, Tony, wouldn't join my church, so I chose to make him a sacrifice. Warren stopped me. I failed my lord, and I want you to help me make it up to *Him* by killing Warren."

Get up and walk away, my rational self was thinking. But my teenage self—you know, the irrational one—decided to get smart. "You're offering me *everything*?"

He nodded. "Whatever demented thing your heart desires, *He* will provide."

"Like he gives you everything?"

Dupree smiled widely. "*He* provides me with all I want."

"So, explain why you're locked up."

His smile faded and his face darkened. "A temporary setback."

"Uh-huh," I said, standing. "I'll pass." I picked up my lunch tray and walked away.

He called after me, "I only have to make good on that sacrifice and the dark lord will open all doors for me." He shouted, "You'll see! One sacrifice will set me free!"

After lights-out that night, as we lay in our bunks, I asked Warren, "How come you didn't tell me that you saved Dupree's cellmate?"

Warren was quiet for a moment. "It was a couple of months before you got here. I woke one night and heard his cellmate wheezing and stuff. I figured Dupree was doing something to him, but I couldn't see in." With our cells next to each other, we were blind as to what our neighbors were up to. "Tony stuck his arm out of their cell right next to ours. I reached through and got a handful of Dupree's hair. Turns out he had cornered Tony by the bars and was strangling him. I banged his head against the bars a few times. I almost knocked him out. He let go of Tony, and by then the guards had shown up."

"Dupree asked me to kill you."

Warren laughed. "Yeah, he's pissed. He went into solitary for a while. Now that he's out I gotta keep my eyes peeled for him. He says he's gonna make me the sacrifice. I'm not worried. Satan's a wimp compared to God."

I finally got my job assignment. I wasn't happy learning I'd work in the morgue.

"I am your boss. You answer to me." Mr. Hoptin was the mortician. He ran his hand over his nearly bald head, slicking back the few hairs that remained. He was round all over—his head, his shoulders. His belly was pudgy-round, and even the thick glasses he wore were circles. "Our job begins after the coroner has confirmed a cause of death. We prepare the body for burial, cremation, or viewing."

His office was well lit, but because the walls and furniture were dark, it was dreary. He'd already shown me the room where the deceased, his preferred term for the dead, were prepared.

He asked if I had questions. "What's in there?" I pointed to a door behind his desk.

"That"—he paused, giving what he said a measure of gravity—"is not your concern. That room is my inner sanctum and is always locked. Do not go in there."

It was pretty gross working with bodies. We stayed busy because the coroner and Mr. Hoptin handled the remains of prisoners throughout the state. Every day Mr. Hoptin brought in a thermos of what he called soup. Funny how it smelled like liquor. Throughout the day he'd take sips, and the more he drank, the more he talked.

"I didn't always work in the penal system," he said one day as we were working on a two-hundred-fifty-pound weight lifter who'd been killed in a riot at a maximum-security prison a couple of hundred miles away. "I had a nice practice going in Ohio, but I had to give up my professional license."

"Why?" I asked as I scrubbed at the dead man's leg.

Mr. Hoptin opened the thermos and took a drink. He bent down and applied makeup to the convict's face; there would be an open-casket ceremony later that day. "I lost my license because of charges that I engaged in inappropriate behavior with my corpses."

What did that mean?

"Why should they care what I do with them? I mean, they're dead, right?" After a moment of silence, I looked up and saw him staring at me. "Right?"

"Yeah," I said, and began the difficult task of putting pants on a large dead person.

Mr. Hoptin sent for two more inmates, and we moved the body into a coffin on a wheeled cart.

He upended his thermos and said, "I'm going to get more soup. Clean up in here."

I wheeled the body to the chapel, then went back and put away the soaps, makeup, brushes, and other tools of the trade. After sweeping and mopping, I went to Mr. Hoptin's office. There was no answer when I knocked, so I went in and saw that the door to his private room—his inner sanctum—was partly open. Curiosity got the better of me, and I tiptoed across the floor and peeked inside.

Mr. Hoptin was at the far side, his back to me. The room was filled with small, round tables of varying heights. Each held a jar of clear liquid. The jars were different sizes, and each was illuminated with track lighting. Something was suspended in the liquid of each jar. Were they pieces of paper? They'd been drawn on. I concentrated on a jar on the table closest to the door. On the parchment was a picture of a heart stabbed by a dagger.

Actually, I thought, *it looks more like a—a tattoo!*

"Ahh, there you are, Carlisle."

I jumped, though Mr. Hoptin didn't seem mad.

"Come in. I don't think you've seen my art gallery, have you?" he slurred.

"Uh, no sir."

He put a finger to his lips. "Shhh, it's a secret." Drunker than I'd ever seen him, he staggered over and pulled me in. "It's a one-of-a-kind collection, I can guarantee that." We stood before the jar I'd been looking at. "That's the classic daggered heart, definitely old school. Over here is a tribal design." He pulled me to a larger jar in which a rectangular piece of flesh eighteen inches long and five inches high was placed. The piece was made up of wavy black lines that artistically meshed with one another. "Got that one off the biceps of a rapist. Funny thing; that tattoo helped the victim identify him."

As he pulled me from tattoo to tattoo, I came to understand that he'd skinned these bits of flesh from dead inmates, suspending them in jars of preservative.

"This shark is by world-renowned Ted Strong." He stumbled to another table. "A Japanese dragon," he mumbled, pointing out a serpentine body. One purple claw held a pipe to its mouth. "It represented the deceased's drug addiction." Mr. Hoptin not only knew the type of tattoos, but the history and artists. "This grabby fellow"— he pointed out a piece of skin on which was tattooed a red octopus with green highlights—"is by another famous artist: Sofia Estrella, formerly Ms. Deborah, formerly Debbie Inksmith. Speaking of famous"—he seized my jumpsuit and rushed me across the room— "look, a Marty Morris," he said reverently. It was a scene from outer space: planets, stars, and meteors on a piece of skin as long as an arm. He sighed. "Those are the gems of my collection. Sadly, most are jailhouse tattoos: poorly designed and poorly applied."

I'd seen enough. "I better get back to my cell."

Mr. Hoptin stepped past me, through the door, and nearly fell into his chair. "Be a good lad and shut off the lights."

I found the light switch three feet in from the doorway and flipped it down.

Mr. Hoptin grabbed my wrist before I got past his desk. "When a particularly good piece from a famous artist makes its way into one of our institutions, I sometimes wish that I could rush that convict's demise so I can gain possession of the artwork."

"D'you mean—"

"Say a marvelous tattoo comes in on someone. Chances are he won't die here." He let go of me and went for another slug of liquor. "At least not before the natural ravages of time fades, blurs, or scars the tattoo." He put his thermos on his desk, stood, and placed his hands on my shoulders. "There is a particular piece on one of the incarcerated lads that I would dearly love to possess. It was created by one of the world's leading masters of black and white, Maxwell Crowley."

I wanted to get away from Mr. Hoptin's sour breath, so I moved around the desk and sat in his guest chair.

He fell back into his seat. "A unique piece, a demon face re-flected in fiery water." He saw my recognition and tried to wink knowingly. "Now, Mr. Carlisle, listen carefully. Should that person suffer, oh, say, a fatal accident, then possession of his tattoo would fall to me. I would certainly be appreciative. In fact, if that hap-pened, I think the rest of your time spent here would be quite easy. Do you get my drift, Mr. Carlisle?"

Amazing. I'd been here for only a short time, and I'd already had two people ask me to kill for them.

His eyelids drooped, and he mumbled, "You'd have to be care-ful not to damage the art while committing the act." His chin fell to his chest. "It's not like anyone would mourn this particular inmate, should anything—any—thi—" He began to snore.

We get an extra hour in the yard on the weekends. There's sports gear: basketball hoops on a half-court, weight-lifting equip-ment, and a volleyball net. I like volleyball and played the following day, a Saturday, until I was a sweaty mess and took a break.

There are picnic tables in the center of the yard, and Warren sat at one reading a book, probably the Bible. I saw Dupree stalking across the yard and heading for the tables. He knelt down and pulled out a thin piece of metal about as big around as a car antenna from his pants leg. It was a foot long, and even at a distance I could tell the end had been sharpened. A shank! He was going after Warren.

I'm not a heroic-type guy, yet some sort of instinct kicked in. My adrenaline started pumping as I ran for the picnic tables. Every-thing became crystal clear, my mind working out the best trajectory to take Dupree down. When he was only steps from Warren, I jumped onto the nearest picnic table and leapt like a super-hero taking flight. Dupree sensed me coming and tried to get the shank up, but I hit him first. We tumbled through the dirt. My head slammed into a table leg, and everything went fuzzy.

Warren helped me up. My head hurt, and when I touched it, my hand came away bloody. The guards swarmed in, taking me to the infirmary, but not before I saw that Dupree had fallen on his shank. It had entered underneath his jaw and pierced through the top of his skull. No one had to worry about Dupree anymore.

I had a concussion, and they kept me in the infirmary for two days. There was an inquiry, but it was pretty open and shut. By the time I went back to work in the morgue, Dupree's body had already been cremated.

Mr. Hoptin was seated at his desk, a happy smile on his face. "You are quite the young man, aren't you?"

"Excuse me?"

"I ask one little favor of you, and you do it the very next day. Impressive."

"It wasn't like that—"

Mr. Hoptin held up his hand. "Tut-tut. We will never again mention the manner in which Jonathan Dupree passed from this world, God rest his soul."

A week later a guard came for me a little before three in the morning. We were navigating the secured corridors before I fully woke.

He led me to the morgue and left me at Mr. Hoptin's office. His chair was turned around so that it faced the door to his art gallery. I cleared my throat, and he jumped as if I'd shouted *boo*.

He whispered, "Come in, Carlisle."

I sat in the other chair.

"You can guess the first thing I did when Jonathan Dupree's body arrived."

I nodded. Mr. Hoptin had skinned the demon face tattoo from Jonathan's chest.

"Have you ever seen those paintings of faces whose eyes follow you no matter where you stand?" He didn't wait for my answer. "The eyes of Dupree's demon do the same. At first I was delighted, but then I noticed other things."

"What other things?"

"Its expression changes!" He nodded as if to verify the statement.

"Maybe it changes if you look at it from some different angles," I offered.

Mr. Hoptin shook his head. "Earlier tonight, it started. I need to know that it's not all in my head."

"What started, Mr. Hoptin?"

He stood and motioned me over. He put a finger to his lips, then moved his ear to the gallery door. I did the same . . . and heard it. Someone was muttering on the other side. It sounded like a mantra, a chant perhaps, maybe a prayer.

"Who's in there?" I whispered.

A frightened smile broke on Mr. Hoptin's sweating face. "Dupree's demon."

For just a moment, the room revolved about me. "It can't be."

"Watch what happens," he whispered, and swung the door open, revealing the darkened room. The chanting instantly stopped.

"Turn on the lights," he ordered.

I remembered the light switch was not by the door but well inside. I would have to lean in or even step inside to reach it. When I shook my head in refusal, Mr. Hoptin pushed me aside. He placed his right hand on the doorframe and reached in with his left. He felt the wall, then leaned in farther. Something grabbed him. One second he was there; the next he gasped and was gone, yanked inside. I stared idiotically at the half-open door and the pitch-black room beyond. My stupor ended at the sound of a struggle, glass breaking, and tables smashed. Mr. Hoptin screamed, and I ran.

I couldn't get far without a key, so I found a dark corner and hid. Hugging my knees, I prayed for help. Then I forced myself up and returned to Mr. Hoptin's dark inner sanctum. The chemical smell of spilled preservative brought tears to my eyes. I heard movement.

"Mr. Hoptin?" I stepped to the light switch, felt for it on the wall, and clicked it up. The lights weren't working.

"Help." His voice was muted, like he had a gag over his mouth.

I ran to his office and rummaged through his desk and found a small flashlight. It didn't work, but I slapped it against my palm, and a weak yellow beam came on. Returning to the tattoo room,

I saw broken jars, overturned tables, and puddles of preservative. Chunks of glass crunched under my feet.

"Mr. Hoptin?"

A faint rasp, something brushing against the floor, came from the far side of the room. I shone the light but could only make out a tangle of twitching shadows.

"Help." His muffled voice had such a quality of despair that I forced myself to cross the room.

Mr. Hoptin lay against the wall, his body convulsing, arms reaching, and legs kicking. It was his body, but not his flesh. From head to foot, Mr. Hoptin was covered by tattoos. Every piece of flesh in his art collection had adhered to his own, and where they met, they made a seam as tight as if sewn. The strip of skin that held the tribal band was wrapped around his calf. The Japanese dragon lay at an angle across his abdomen. The octopus covered an arm and Dupree's demon—the demon tattoo had mounted itself right over Mr. Hoptin's face. The skin hugged so tight that I could see the round outline of Mr. Hoptin's glasses stretching out and distorting the tattooed demon's eyes.

"Can't breathe." The tattooed mouth of the demon moved in and out as Mr. Hoptin tried to draw air. He made futile attempts to pull the tattoo from his face, but his hands wore cumbersome flesh mittens. My eyes were drawn to an area above his foot. It wasn't covered. I heard squishy movement and saw the small bit of flesh with the daggered heart wiggle across the floor like an inchworm.

It squirmed up his foot, covered the open space, and melded with the other tattoos.

I turned to run but tripped over a broken table and smacked my head on the floor. Stunned, but still conscious and still grasping the flashlight, I lifted the light to see Mr. Hoptin's skin-shrouded body, the hideous face of Dupree's demon leering down at me. Every few seconds one of the bits of flesh wiggled and stretched, resituating itself with a wet sound. In his skin-mittened hand, the patchwork man held a long sliver of glass from one of the broken jars. It placed the glass shard against the tattooed mouth of the demon and, making a sound like ripping fabric, sliced open the preserved flesh. The figure smacked its new-made lips and spoke—spoke in Jonathan Dupree's voice.

"I told you that a sacrifice would set me free."

I lost consciousness as Dupree's demon shambled from the room.

"I've just figured out that Lucinda isn't a girl I'd want to be alone with in the dark," Demarius said.

Millie caught me watching as she rubbed at her arms. "Goose bumps."

"Wrapped in other people's skin," I thought out loud and shivered.

"Hey—where's Mr. Tremblin?" Millie asked, putting the *Book of Daemon Hall* on the desk next to the lantern.

Time had slowed during the story, and it remained dark. One candle didn't do much to dispel the gloom in that house, and Ian Tremblin was nowhere within the lantern's reach.

We heard shuffling and Ian Tremblin spoke, his voice deep and rasping, "I love a story where evil triumphs."

Why was he cloaking himself in darkness? "What are you doing, Mr. Tremblin?"

"I find the end of that story much more satisfying than the others. For instance, Little Fox kills the great beast? Bah, she should have been butchered and consumed."

I looked in the direction he spoke from, but only saw a veil of black.

"Evil didn't win in Lucinda's story," Millie said, looking this way and that. "Jonathan Dupree died."

"But his demon lived." There was a thump as Ian Tremblin took a step closer, and I could just make out the pale skin of his face. "Which is better than the ambiguous finale of 'The Go-To Guy.' Lobotomize that boy!" His voice rose, and he took another step. "And Dante should have lost his soul, not just a hand." He spoke so forcefully that he sprayed spittle. "I heard all your stories! And only Lucinda's had a proper finish!" Another step and he was within the circle of candlelight, standing at attention, face ahead, only his flat eyes moving, traveling from Millie, to Demarius, to me.

"Mr. Tremblin?" I said. "Is there anything you want to tell us?"

"Yes. I want you to rewrite your stories and to end them suitably."

"The password, Mr. Tremblin?" Millie said hoarsely. "What's the password?"

"Password?" His blank face convulsed and settled on a smile. "Open-says-a-me?"

"What's the real password?" Demarius begged.

"Shave-and-a-haircut? Olly-olly-oxen-free? Alpha-tango-foxtrot?" Ian Tremblin moved toward us, spreading his arms as if preparing to hug us all.

"Go!" I shouted, and we rushed out the door into the black hallway.

Unable to see, I held out my right hand to feel along the wall while grasping Millie with my left. Demarius was just in front of me. Ian Tremblin laughed. It started low, rose in pitch, and continued in a shrill scream.

No longer cautious, we ran.

Demarius stood in utter darkness. Wade and Millie had been right behind him when they fled Tremblin, but when he finally stopped he was alone. He wasn't even sure he stood on solid ground anymore. In this darkness Demarius felt like he was floating, perhaps in the middle of the ocean on a black night, and then he remembered what Lucinda had said earlier about sharks and stomped his foot, making sure solid ground was under him.

"Helloooo!" His shout carried no echo; the darkness swallowed sound. "Where are you guys?" No one answered.

He held up a hand and couldn't see it. He felt totally vulnerable in the dark, and his fear ratcheted up a notch, until he was imagining noises all around him. *Something could be right next to me*, he thought, *and I wouldn't be able to tell.* He shook his head, trying to get it together, and then remembered the candle Wade had given him. Matches too. He dug it out of his pocket. For a moment he thought he'd lost the matches and flint, then he found them pushed into the corner of another pocket.

"Oh, yeah," he said in a shaky voice. "Let there be light." He struck the match and got a feeble spark. It flared on the next try, and he lit the candlewick. He sighed with relief. "I'm in a hall-way." He saw another flickering glow way down the hall—he'd found someone! He raised his candle high. "Hey! Hey, I'm here!"

Whoever it was raised a candle, too, but didn't answer. He started toward the light, and his candle nearly went out, so he cupped a hand in front of the flame. The person with the other candle also put a hand in front of theirs.

"Awww, man." He knew where he was. Last year they had marveled at the depth of the house by standing at the entrance of a first-floor hallway that had a mirror at the other end. They held up a lantern, and the mirror had reflected the tiniest pin-prick of light. That's where he was. His thoughts turned to the others, and his concern for them turned into profound worry. Matt and Lucinda were first-timers in Daemon Hall; they didn't know what they were in for. He hoped they still had each other.

"I'm over here." A female voice spoke so calmly that it didn't startle him.

"Millie? Lucinda?"

"This way," the voice said matter-of-factly.

Demarius could barely discern a figure in the dark, just outside one of the doorways. He started toward her, and she stepped inside.

"Wait."

"In here."

"What?" Demarius stopped at the door. "What's in there?" He extended his arm, putting the candle in the room. He could make out nearby furnishings and framed pictures on the closest wall. Someone grabbed his wrist. He inhaled in shock, breathing in a sweet perfume that immediately calmed him. He was pulled gently into the room, and his knees went weak as he stared down into eyes as blue as Caribbean waters.

"Hi, Demarius," Narcissa Daemon said.

He gulped. "You—you know my name?"

Smiling, she took the candle from his hand and tilted it over a small table, dropping gobs of wax. She stuck the candle to it and wrapped her arms around his waist. He stared into her mesmerizing eyes and felt as though he and Narcissa were spinning around the room in a passionate dance. She placed a hand on his chest, seeming to relish the feel of his hammering heart.

"Kiss me."

"What? No! You're—you're—"

Her smile widened, and she ran a hand down the front of a white gauzy nightgown that hugged her perfect figure. It was low cut, so her cleavage rose and fell with deep breaths. He knew then that they'd been wrong about her. The house showed them lies; she had not killed her family. She was beautiful, innocent, and alive.

"I've watched you," she said. "Each time you've come, I watch from a distance. I can't take my eyes from you. I need more, Demarius. I need you." She moved her arms around his neck and pulled him down to her waiting lips. "Be mine."

Demarius lowered his head to kiss her but stopped when he heard movement elsewhere. He saw shadowy forms.

"Someone's here."

"They're my friends," Narcissa said. "Gentlemen, meet Demarius."

At least a dozen men moved from the gloom into the candle glow. The oldest was close to eighty, and the youngest was a boy of eleven or twelve. The clothes they wore seemed to highlight fashion changes through the decades. Demarius recognized styles he'd seen in old black-and-white movies. One long-haired guy with a peace symbol T-shirt could have come straight from Demarius's story, "The Go-To Guy." He judged the most recent to be a teen wearing a sideways cap and jeans so baggy that he held the waist to keep them up.

Narcissa stroked Demarius's cheek, getting his attention while sending all kinds of good feelings through his body. Yet when he looked back at the group, jealousy blossomed until his fury felt righteous.

He turned his burning gaze back to Narcissa. "Your boyfriends?"

She placed a finger to his lips. "No, silly. They're friends, that's all. You're my lover and can stay with me forever."

Somewhere in his mind he wondered whether she'd said the same thing to each of those men, but as her finger rested on his mouth, his rage departed.

She took away her finger and moved her face close. Their lips almost touched, and she whispered, "You can have me if you promise to always be mine." She kissed him. It was no chaste peck on the lips, but a deep, spellbinding pleasure. Her lips sent electricity racing over his flesh and through his nerves. His eyes rolled back in his head, and he grabbed her, pushing her body tight against his. Her tongue darted and tickled, teasing and delightfully torturing in all that it implied. She pulled from his lips and gave him a seductive smile. Breathing hard, Demarius wanted more—no, he needed it. He pushed against her mouth so forcefully her teeth cut his lip.

She pushed him back and brushed his lips with an index finger, holding it so he could see his blood there. She put her finger in her mouth, consuming what he bled. He moaned, and she delighted in his response.

She took his hand and pulled him before a full-size mirror. "See us?"

Staring at their reflection, he nodded. Her arms encircled one of his. They were stunning together. She was perfect, and he'd never noticed before, but he was good-looking, downright handsome as he stood at her side.

"That can be us always. All you have to do is say you'll be mine forever."

His head still woozy from their kiss, Demarius nodded. "I—"

He noticed movement to his right, quickly glanced over, and saw the old man with a hand on the boy's shoulder. They stared at Demarius with pleading eyes; the boy subtly shook his head. Demarius turned his gaze back to the mirror.

"Will—"

What had gone on before, what would happen later, didn't matter. Having the most beautiful woman he'd ever seen was the only important thing. He gazed spellbound at her reflected beauty and the erotic promise in her smile.

"Stay with—"

He stared harder and breathed in her perfume.

"You—"

He felt drunk from the fragrance.

"For—"

Something cut through her sweet smell and assaulted his nose like a fart in church.

"For—"

The odor was terrible. Through sheer force of will, he looked from her mirror image to her. He tried to shout, to scream, but all he managed was a guttural sound. The lips that he'd kissed seconds before had turned into a festering mouth ravaged with

sores. He tried pulling from her grasp, but Narcissa, now a tangle of putrid flesh and white bones, gripped his arm tighter.

"Kiss me!" she gurgled.

"NO!" he shrieked, and yanked himself free.

Laughing, she cooed appreciatively at her reflection and patted her hair with a skeletal hand, not seeming to notice when clumps fell to the floor. In the mirror was a remarkably beautiful young woman, but the real her, the one he'd kissed, turned to him and the skin on her nose split, revealing cartilage and wet nasal passages.

He screamed shrilly and snatched the candle from the table as he ran past to the hall. After only a few steps, he tripped and fell. The candle landed in front of him and went out. He choked back another scream. In the dark, too scared to move, he listened. There was no sound of pursuit, no noise at all, except for his rapid breathing. Reaching out hesitantly, he felt along the floor, retrieved his candle, and relit it with shaking hands. Except for himself, the hallway was deserted. He pushed himself up and felt something in his mouth. He held up a hand and spat it out. It looked like a grain of plump rice. Had he eaten rice at that Italian restaurant? He didn't think so. Staring harder, he figured out what it was when it wiggled. He gagged and ran down the hallway so fast the candle went out.

Even so, he didn't slow.

Millie ran it through her head again. When she had finished reading Lucinda's self-writing story, Mr. Tremblin had changed. It was like Wade had written in his book—the writer and Daemon Hall became one. They all ran from Tremblin, of course. One second she held Wade's hand; the next, she grasped air. She didn't know where she was, but stumbled against a chair and sat. Millie called out. No one answered, and she lit the candle Wade had given her. She'd somehow made it back to Daemon's study. There was a *squeak-creak* from above, and she tried to convince herself that it was only the sound of the old house settling. When it came again, she admitted it sounded more like a rope from which something heavy was suspended. She refused to look up, knowing she'd see Mr. Daemon swinging like a pendulum. She sat unmoving, rooted by fear—the high-octane variety.

Someone screamed. It was distant and sounded like it came from one of the floors below her. Her concern for her friends gave her the courage to move. She stood, picked up the *Book of Daemon Hall*, and without looking up, left the room.

She moved slowly to keep the candle lit, but that was okay because she didn't know where to go. She decided to look in all the places they'd already been: the second-floor study, downstairs library, entrance hall, dining room, and kitchen.

She thought about Wade. Something was developing between them. He was handsome, white hair and all, as well as smart and funny. She had to admit another attraction was how damaged he was. He had anxiety attacks, had been shut away in a mental institution, and worst of all, had been permanently scarred by Daemon Hall. Why did that appeal to her? Then it hit her. It wasn't what he'd been through—it was how he handled it. In spite of it all, he was, well, Wade. Most people would be a paranoid bundle of nerves. To survive all he had, and to be like he was, took more determination and bravery than she could imagine.

More desperate now to find Wade, all of them, Millie rushed down the hallway, passing the master bedroom suite. Cornelia's door was open to a dark still room. The twins' door was closed, and when she stepped by, she heard a click. She abruptly stopped—from the corner of her eye she saw the door swing half open.

Standing across the hall, she called, "Is someone there? Wade?"

She heard a rhythmic slapping that took her back to child-hood, when she would kneel while facing her best friend, Chloë Jenkins, and recite,

> Pat-a-cake, pat-a-cake, baker's man.
> Bake me a cake as fast as you can.
> Pat it and roll it and mark it with a "B"
> and put it in the oven for baby and me.

They'd quickly moved on to the more complicated rhythms of claps and slaps, which opened up a whole new vista of creative rhymes.

> I'm a little hottie, of that there is no doubt.
> All the boys at my school, would like to ask me out.

Another came to her.

> One bright day in the middle of the night,
> two dead boys got up to fight.
> Back to back they faced each other,
> drew their swords and shot each other.
> A deaf policeman heard the noise
> and ran to save the two dead boys.
> And if you don't believe it's true,
> ask the blind man—he saw it too.

Two dead boys? Her thoughts were interrupted by two young voices reciting with the hand-clap rhythm.

I am outside playing, running with my pup
Mommy is upon the porch, calling me to sup.
"Mother, may I stay out, play a little more?"
"Just a few more minutes, then come in through this door."

Millie took a step closer, holding out her candle.

Later, Mommy strokes my cheek, says, "It's time for bed,"
I yawn and nearly fall asleep when pillow meets my head.
Mother starts a story with, "Once a beanstalk grew,"
But I'm fast in slumber land before the story's through.

Millie used her toe to push the door fully open. The room was filled with sharp-edged shadows. Her candle illuminated the Daemon twins, pale and listless, kneeling on a round carpet in the center of the room, joylessly beating out rhythms on their chests, thighs, and hands.

Something wakes me later, something that sounds near.
I tiptoe quietly down the hall so Mommy will not hear,
Slipping out the front door, into the midnight dew,
greeting the town's children, out in a dark night blue.

Someone leads us dancing, to that tall black tree,
and we climb like monkeys, laughing merrily.
Halfway up that tall black tree we find a big, wide crack,
and we climb inside the tree into a darkness black.

Millie gasped. Earlier they'd discussed the mystery of the children who vanished hundreds of years ago from the little village that was built upon Oaskagu. Somehow she knew that was what the dead twins chanted about.

> *Deep inside the tree now, no longer having fun.*
> *We cry and scream and can't get out, there's nowhere*
> > *we can run.*
> *I wish I hadn't snuck out, I'm sorry that I came,*
> *there's something creeping closer now, it's calling me*
> > *by name.*

Their final clap came with the last word. Millie stared, mesmerized.

"It's calling me by name," they repeated, and turned to her. "It's calling YOU by name." Each lifted a hand in perfect synchronicity to point at her. "Millie!"

She fled down the hallway, not daring to slow even when she dropped her candle.

Millie wondered how long she'd been inside Daemon Hall. It seemed forever. But how could you measure the passage of time when it kept speeding up? Since they had gone way back to 1933, did that mean they'd spent decades in Daemon Hall? Or should they judge by how time passed for them, which she figured could be measured in hours? That seemed more plausible, considering she hadn't had a thing to eat since the restaurant and was just starting to feel hunger. Her friends would be hungry too, she thought, concerned for their well-being. She was particularly worried about Matt. He was the youngest and had been the most frightened. She walked faster, knowing that all she could do was search.

She ached, knowing she must have some impressive bruises. After her encounter with the twins, she'd been so frightened that she'd run blindly. During her flight she ran into a wall, bouncing back like she'd hit a vertical trampoline. At least it brought her to her senses. By that time she was lost. Still was. Nothing seemed familiar. She didn't even know what floor she was on. Was it still the third? She couldn't remember stairs, but then she didn't recall much from her panicked dash. Through it all she'd miraculously managed to hang on to the *Book of Daemon Hall*. She kept mainly to the hallways. Her eyes adjusted enough that she could see for a couple of feet, but when she looked into doorways as she passed, the rooms were too dark to see inside. More than once Millie wondered if her heart had stopped when the twins screamed her name and she was now a ghost wandering Daemon Hall forever. Where were her friends? She called out Wade's name, but the house absorbed her voice.

She turned a corner and saw a glimmering light, a candle held chest high. Her initial reaction had been to run and see who it was, but after her playdate with the twins, she'd be extra-cautious. She started for the candle. Keeping her eyes on the diminutive flame, she stubbed her toe on a short flight of four stairs—the hallway rose here. Slowly ascending, she realized the candle wasn't chest high, but on the floor, and she could discern a figure lying next to it.

"Hello?" she called softly, noticing that her voice quavered. The figure didn't answer, and she took a couple more steps. "It's me, Millie."

"Muhhhh," was the reply.

"Are you okay?"

"Noooooo."

Millie stopped a second. "Wade?" She rushed over, knelt beside him, and put down the *Book of Daemon Hall*. His candle had been set in a glob of wax but looked ready to topple. Millie picked it up, dripped more wax, and reseated it. "Wade? Can you hear me?"

He looked terrible. He lay on his side, hugging his knees. His body twitched; his eyes darted back and forth. A white froth leaked from his mouth.

"Wade? Can you hear me? I'm right here."

"Muhhhh—Millie?"

Relief flowed through her. "I'm here." She stroked his cheek. "You're not alone."

"Nuhhh 'lone. I was wuh-worried about you—scared for you."

"Shhh, I'm okay. Is it an attack, Wade? Are you having a panic attack?"

He twitched on the floor. "Buh—bad one."

Millie started to tell him to let the attack run its course, but it was obvious that his fits were painful and frightening. Other than a theory based on ancestral superstition, what reason did she have to ask that of him? But even now, full of doubt, it seemed right. She'd always been intuitive, and her instinct still said Wade should seek a vision. Knowing it would haunt her forever if something happened to him, she said, "Wade, don't fight it."

"Wha—"

"Remember what I said earlier? How the Nanticoke honored those who had attacks like you're having."

"Yuh—yes."

"They had visions, epiphanies. I know you hate it by how hard you fight, but if somehow there was a chance it could help us, wouldn't it be worth it?"

Wade struggled to look at her. "Nuh worth it."

"I know some of the old Native American beliefs can seem strange. But what if there's something to them, what if they were right about having visions? I wouldn't ask if I didn't think it might help."

Wade shook his head violently. "Can't!"

"Wade, you can. There's a big connection between where we are, in Daemon Hall—on Oaskagu—and my people. Don't fight it, don't stop it. You might see a way out. I'll be here, Wade. I'll watch over you and keep you safe."

For a moment his shaking stopped and his eyes turned up to her. He gave an almost imperceptible nod and shut his eyes. The trembling renewed. Spasms that originated deep inside him multiplied until he was vibrating on the floor.

Anxiety attacks are a paradoxical circle. Sufferers are scared of them, yet they're sometimes triggered by the fear of having one. My therapist says for most people, they begin subtly and build from there. I've had those wimpy starters, but mostly I'm blind-sided. They come out of nowhere and strike me like a city bus doing fifty-five.

I remembered Millie reading Lucinda's perverse story, followed by Ian Tremblin not knowing the password, which of course meant he wasn't really Ian Tremblin. He came after us; we ran. I held tight to Millie, but not tight enough. Daemon Hall was good at separating people and getting them alone. Though terrified for myself, I worried more about my friends, and ago-nized over Millie's safety. I wandered, not quite blindly, thanks to my little candle, when all at once it felt like I got sucker punched. Wheezing for air, I was burning up, perspiring heavily, and then the chills started. I fell, shivering in a vise of pain and fear. My candle rolled against the wall, nearly dying. Even in the throes of a strong attack, I managed to pick up the candle and stick it in wax that had spilled.

I'd discovered that if I could keep everything outside of me from having any influence, then I could concentrate on fighting my way out of an attack from within. To do that, I shut down my senses until it was only me, safely tucked into my subconscious cocoon. I didn't hear, see, feel, taste, or smell anything. Then something on the outside made it through to the inner me. I pushed my way to consciousness, which was like floating up through gradually thinning smoke, until I saw Millie kneeling over me.

She asked something crazy of me and stroked my face. I did what she wanted; I let the attack come on full force. I sank into the inner me again, but it was different this time; I was standing in the dark somewhere in my subconscious. It seemed real. Two objects glowed in a haze before coming into focus. One was a tree that had a dark radiance, and it grew so high I couldn't see the top. Straight ahead, a good distance away, was Millie. A whitish glimmering surrounded her. She stared at me as she lifted a bow and arrow. She pulled back the bowstring and shot the arrow straight at me. Though fear or panic would have been appropriate emotions, all I felt was bewilderment as the arrow flew at my heart.

I opened my eyes and gazed up at Millie. My head in her lap, she massaged my temples while singing a wordless tune that sounded Native American.

"Hi," I croaked.

"Wade? How do you feel?"

"Like I went through a wood chipper."

"Is it over?"

"Yeah."

Her fingers went to work on my temples. "Well? Did you— you know—"

"Have a vision?" I sat up and gave her a weak smile.

She looked at me with wide-eyed wonder. "Really?"

"Really."

"What did you see?"

"I saw you shoot a bow and arrow."

"I did what?"

"Actually, you shot me with the bow and arrow." I went on to tell her everything I'd envisioned.

She took my hand. "You know how crazy that was?"

"I know."

"I'd never hurt you. I like you—I like you a lot."

It was a good thing I was already sitting; otherwise, that admission would've knocked me to the ground. "It's just something I saw in my head during a panic attack."

"Yeah."

"And I like you, too."

We stared at each other, grinning like idiots.

"I'm sorry I asked you to do that."

"Just a dream," I repeated.

"I was so worried about you." Millie's voice broke. She threw her arms around my neck and hugged me.

"I was scared for you, too."

We pulled apart.

"The others," she said.

I nodded, getting to my feet. "Let's find them."

My stub of a candle provided our light. I took my wallet and flipped it open. I used wax to attach the candle to one side, then held up the other to act as a wind guard. Millie carried the *Book of Daemon Hall.*

"Where are we?" she asked. "I mean in time. *When* are we?"

"The way night and day keep racing by, I'd say decades have passed."

We emerged from a hall onto the second-floor landing. I sat on the top step.

"Wade? We don't have time to rest."

"No, I have to tell the last story, 'The Leaving.'" I patted the floor beside me. "After I make a confession to you."

She sat and put the book on my lap. "Confession?"

I took a deep breath. "Whatever shows up in here"—I tapped the book—"won't be anything I wrote."

"How do you know that?"

"Because I didn't write a story."

"What?"

I stared at the floor since I couldn't look her in the eye. "I lied to you, to Ian Tremblin, to everybody. Mr. Tremblin gave me the title, yeah, but no matter how hard I tried, I couldn't come up with anything. I should have told the truth earlier, but each time I lied, it got harder to 'fess up. I'm sorry, Millie."

"It's okay. Writer's block probably happens to all writers at one time or another."

"Well, it never happened to me before. And it was more like writer's vacuum. There wasn't anything there. It was as though I had a history report to write on some event that hadn't happened yet."

"Why was it so easy for us and hard for you?"

"I have a theory. And I think Mr. Tremblin was on to it before he changed." I held up the *Book of Daemon Hall*. "This was made from paper pulped from the black tree, right? That makes the book as much a part of Daemon Hall as its cornerstone. I'll bet there are a lot more stories, but it chooses which to share, which to bring to a page. We've only seen the few relevant to us. My guess is that every terrible thing that's happened in Daemon Hall and Oaskagu is recorded here. I don't think any of you actually wrote the stories. They were already in here, not visible as written words, but in here just the same. Daemon Hall used you to release them."

"How? I was far away from the book when I wrote my story—we all were."

"Once Ian Tremblin assigned those titles, the book gained influence over you. If Daemon Hall can bend time for its benefit, why not distance? That's why everyone had such an easy time with those stories."

"It didn't influence you. You didn't write anything."

"That's right, but I bet that if I start reading it, something will happen."

Millie took the book and stared at it. After a moment, she groaned, flipped pages, and stopped at the title "The Leaving." She pushed the book onto my lap.

I cleared my throat and said, " 'The Leaving,' by Wade Reilly."

Words written in elegant cursive appeared under the title, and I read along. " 'Wade and Millie descend the staircase to the great entrance hall. It's there that they have the slightest chance to discover the means of their leaving—but, in all probability, will only encounter the method of their death.' "

No other words appeared.

"That's all?" Millie frantically grabbed the book and shook it like an Etch A Sketch. "Come on, give us more."

I took it from her. "That's all there is. 'The Leaving' is our story. Get it? There's no more to read because the story's not finished. It starts with us going down there." I pointed to the entrance hall. "It will write itself as it happens."

Millie is the bravest girl I've ever known. Still, she was so afraid that she was close to tears. In a broken voice, she asked, "Instead of reading it, we have to live it?"

"I hope there's a happy ending." That lame excuse for a joke brought a small smile to her lips, and I knew right then that I would do anything to protect her.

"If 'The Leaving' is our story—if it's real—what about the other ones?" She pointed at the book. "'A Promise for Bones,' 'The Go-To Guy,' those really happened?"

I stood. "They're not fictional stories—they're historical accounts."

I helped Millie up, and though we were frightened, we started down the great staircase. The candle stub sputtered out halfway down, and I shoved it in my pocket. But we could still see. A bluish haze, like the soft ocean glow created by phosphorescent algae, rose from the marble floor.

"Daemon Hall wants us to see what's coming," Millie whispered.

"That's probably not a good thing."

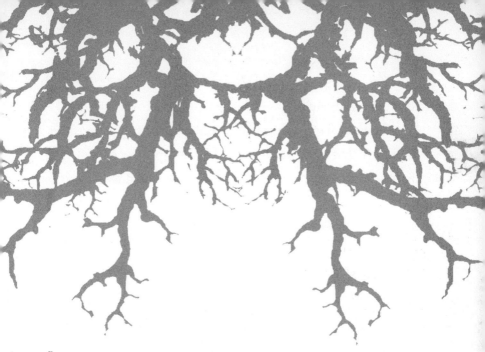

In the house a man wandered alone. Often he stumbled aimlessly; occasionally he ran. Sometimes he looked for the teens so he could kill them; other times he hid for fear that he might do that very thing. A battle raged in his mind, heart, and soul. It was a fight for control, for identity, and for his being. He was tired and sweaty, but his enemy didn't diminish its fight for his body, and neither could he. For a long time, the relentless combat had been internal, but finally, as the bearded man's resolve broke, the fight became externally evident. He weaved, contorted, and bounced from the walls, speaking gibberish.

"Mine. You are mine!" A growl, not his voice, came from his mouth.

"No—nev—never. You will not—not hurt them," he answered, words slurred with exhaustion.

"You will rip, you will rend, you will tear them to pieces!"

"Go—go to hell!"

The man slapped himself with his right hand. Almost immediately that blow was answered by a slap from his left. The man sneered, eyes crossed as he tried to look at himself, and his right hand balled into a fist that flew into his chin, rocking his head back and sending his glasses flying.

"Leave my body!" he shouted.

His left fist hit him squarely in the middle of his face.

"Never."

He knew what was at stake. He had to fight even if it took hours, days, decades. If Daemon Hall got him now, his soul and the lives of his young friends would be lost. He couldn't stop, wouldn't, even if his heart quit from fatigue. The muttering, the shouts, the blows, and the blood continued as Ian Tremblin stumbled through the dark hallways.

Since we were the characters in "The Leaving," we descended the stairs as described in the narrative. The entire entrance hall was visible in the blue glow. As our feet touched the marble floor, things began to shake. At first it was a mild vibration, but the intensity increased until the whole hall rumbled.

Millie lost her balance and grabbed at me, shouting, "What's happening?"

"I don't know!"

The quake strengthened, and we had trouble keeping on our feet. The floor rippled like it was made of rubber. Millie screamed as one violent roll sent her stumbling. Across the surging floor, near the front of the house, an explosion hurled chunks of shattered marble and splintered lumber into the air.

The debris rained down and I threw up my arms. "Look out!"

There was a hole in the floor, a crater, where the explosion had originated, from which something climbed into view. Black, with twisted limbs, it had stiletto-pointed branches.

As I watched it rise through the floor, its name fell from my lips: "Oaskaguakw."

Millie, hands over her ears, stared at the expanding tree. Then I encountered something that scared me more than anything I'd seen so far—her courage broke. Screaming, she turned and raced up the staircase, leaving me behind on the thrashing floor. I tried to make my way to the stairs, but the ground buckled and I flew in the opposite direction. It was too turbulent to stand, so I lay flat while watching limbs bigger around than a weight lifter's torso expand and push out. Bumps erupted on the limbs, then sprouted and produced buds, which got big and formed bizarre shapes. They grew larger still, unveiling bodies that dangled from the branches.

Still growing, the tree punctured the ceiling, and chunks of the roof fell in. I rolled away as a slab crashed where I'd been a moment before. The quake lessened, and I pushed to my knees. The treetop was through the ceiling, and branches punched out the walls. The tree had reclaimed its place.

Upon those branches were dozens of suspended bodies— seventy, eighty, maybe more. And I knew who they were. A mishmash of emotions ran through me as I took inventory of the tree's crop: fear, revulsion, sympathy, compassion. Scattered among the limbs were those who had died during the construction of Daemon Hall. Many were twisted by the disease that eventually snapped their spines. Twenty feet overhead was what looked like an overstuffed figure with a demon's face, its outer flesh patched in brightly colored tattoos. To the other side of the tree and farther up, hung the great beast from Millie's story. A man who would barely draw a glance if seen out on the street hung higher; I recognized him as Demarius's Go-To Guy. Far above, gathered in a sad little clump of five, were the Daemons. And the others? Judging from their nightclothes, the scattered children were the ones who had disappeared from the small village that was once located on Oaskagu. The rest, I supposed, were thrill seekers who had come and never left.

I heard the rapid slap of feet against stone; Millie flew down the stairs. She'd come back!

"Wade! Little Fox did leave this!" She held up the bow from the glass case in Daemon's study. "Remember in my story? She buried her weapons in case a warrior needed them to fight the Oaskagu evil. It's real! It's history!"

Was Millie that warrior? She ran closer to the tree, then stopped and fumbled to set the arrow in the bowstring.

There was a thump and another: The fruit had ripened. Bodies dropped, then stood.

Millie pulled back on the bow and aimed at Oaskaguakw, then shifted to the figures spawned by the tree. The flesh eater of the Nanticoke plunged to the floor not twenty feet from her. It was on all fours, sniffing the air.

"Oh God, oh God, oh God." Her voice trembled.

The arrow slipped from the bowstring and fell to the floor. She squatted and felt for it while keeping her eyes on the beast. She found the arrow at the exact moment the great beast fixed on her and stretched its oversized mouth into a daggered grin. She yelped, and the monster's grin split its face even more.

"Wade?" Millie called desperately. The beast circled her. She spun, notched the arrow, and screamed, "There's only one arrow!"

I wanted to shout something that would help, or run over and defend her, but I was numb with fear and paralyzed by terror. Other things dropped from the tree and started for Millie. I had also attracted unwanted attention, including the Satanic tattooed patchwork from Lucinda's story.

"Wade!" Millie shrieked, gazing helplessly at me, tears on her cheeks. I watched her expression change—her eyes narrowed. She gritted her teeth, lifted the bow, and sighted. This was all so familiar, damn near a déjà-vu. Why? And why was the arrow aimed at me?

I found my voice. "Millie! What are you doing?"

"Your vision," she shouted, like that would explain everything. It hardly seemed real in that bluish haze as she pulled the bowstring all the way back.

"Millie?"

Terrified, she cried, "It's what I have to do!"

"What do you have to—"

She didn't seem to hear me. Nor did she see the great beast turn abruptly and charge at her. She didn't see the dozens of creatures rushing in its wake. She wasn't aware of anything except the bow and arrow, and her target—me.

"No, Millie! Don't!"

She released the bowstring as the beast knocked her screaming to the ground. The missile cut through the air: halfway across the foyer, three-quarters of the way, and I stood at ground zero. I felt the impact as the arrow drove home—into the *Book of Daemon Hall* that I held in front of my chest. Four inches of the shaft stuck out the back, stopping a quarter of an inch from my ribs. In shock, I fell to my knees.

All around us, the creatures, beasts, and monsters borne by Oaskaguakw stopped and collapsed to the floor. Millie kicked away the corpse of the flesh eater and stood. Within seconds all the bodies had decomposed, turning to greasy puddles that streamed over the floor like mercury and spilled into the hole at the base of the tree.

Millie threw down the bow and ran across the broken floor. "Wade? Wade? Are you okay?" She knelt before me, tears on her cheeks, and ran her hands over my face, arms, and chest, making sure I was still whole.

All I could say was "Great shot."

It was faint at first, a crackle of surging energy coming from Oaskaguakw. The sound built in volume, then rose to a crescendo that could be felt, like a lightning blast that strikes too close. Still kneeling, we grabbed each other and watched open-mouthed as the black tree imploded. It collapsed upon itself and disappeared in a goopy spray of reddish-black liquid that sounded like a summer shower as splats fell to the farthest corners of the entrance hall. It smelled rancid, like putrefying meat.

Millie and I stared at each other. The tree was gone. The marble floor was in one piece, as were the ceiling and walls. Then Millie faded from sight as the subtle glow went out.

"I thought you were shooting *me*." I'd relit my candle stub and worked the arrow free from the *Book of Daemon Hall.* "Here, in case you need it again."

Something fell from the book and glided to the floor. It was a piece of paper, I assumed a page torn free by the piercing arrow.

Millie picked it up and handed it to me. "I remembered your vision, and when I saw you with the book, it made sense."

I sat on the bottom step to catch my breath and folded the paper. I'd been an avid paper airplane maker when I was a kid. My specialty was a streamlined and pointy-nosed design that flew through the air with almost as much precision as Millie's arrow. Without my really paying attention, one of those was taking form in my hands. "At least you're a good shot."

"Uh, actually, I've never shot a bow and arrow," Millie

confessed, sitting next to me. "Somehow I knew I wouldn't miss, something to do with Little Fox's bow."

We rested for several minutes. I hefted the plane. The paper was heavy, and it would fly well, but I didn't throw it. It probably wasn't a good idea to practice origami with paper made from Oaskaguakw, much less start throwing it around. I shoved the airplane into the middle of the book and shut it.

"Wade, outside!"

Time shifted into overdrive, and we watched the windows as day and night alternated. It was hypnotic. Light. Dark. Light. Dark. When that metallic rasp of slowing time interrupted, day remained. We grinned at each other. Millie was covered in goo from the tree. I was too.

She wiped a handful of the reddish-black gunk from my hair. "Ugh, you stink." We laughed as she tried to shake it from her hands.

"My new cologne, eau de roadkill."

There was a clack and rattling across the foyer. The front door swung wide. A group of people stood outside the entrance. They came in cautiously and shut the door.

Millie mumbled, "What . . . ?" Then, "It's you."

Along with Demarius, Chris and Kara. They—we—carried four large gas cans.

"Oh, no," I whispered. "We've shown up to set the house on fire."

Millie gripped my arm, disbelief thick in her voice.

"Daemon Hall rushed us through time so the fire you start will kill us."

"We need to find everyone and leave." My voice shook as we took the stairs two at a time. "We stay together no matter what. We'll run through the house and yell for them. I don't know how much time we have because strange things happened before we set the fire—an hour at most."

We'd just started down the second-floor hall when the grinding noise of slowing time reverberated through the house.

"Time jumped again." Millie had an edge of panic in her voice.

"Which means we have even less time."

She handed me her watch so that I could keep track of how much time passed while she kept the bow and arrow ready. We saw someone crouched in a corner in one room, absolute terror on his face. It was me from before, when we'd arrived to set the fire. Back then the noise made us panic, and this is where I ended up. The other me in the corner glanced up. I remembered when I saw vague shapes through the doorway and thought they were ghosts. I guess, in a way, I was haunting myself.

"Go away!" that other me shouted. "Leave me alone!"

I pulled Millie away. "Come on."

"But, he needs—you need—help."

"That me will be fine. It's this one"—I poked my chest—"that I'm worried about."

On the third floor, after shouting, we miraculously got an

answer. Most everybody rounded a corner, exhausted, scared, and in shock. Lucinda and Demarius smiled, but Matt didn't. He kept one foot off the ground while leaning against Demarius. We gathered for a long moment in a group hug.

"Gross!" Lucinda pulled away. "What's that slime all over you guys?"

"Where's Mr. Tremblin?" I asked.

Demarius shook his head. "Haven't seen him."

Millie filled them in on the four gas-toting teens, including Demarius and me, that we had seen enter Daemon Hall. "We need to get out right now. The fire happens soon."

"Millie and I think some of this is about revenge. The house wants to make sure we're here when it goes up."

Millie nodded. "So we have to find Mr. Tremblin as soon as possible."

"What if he's still possessed or whatever?" Demarius asked.

"Look, I'm not saying we leave him, but our first priority should be to get out before the place burns up." I pointed to the front of the house. "If we're lucky, we'll come across him on the way."

I directed a question at Lucinda. "What happened in Daemon's office after the door closed?"

Lucinda said that after Daemon died, time had shifted and the door opened. She and Matt couldn't find anyone. They blindly roamed the house until Demarius literally ran into them while escaping from Narcissa. The collision sprained Matt's ankle. They'd climbed to the third floor in search of us. Millie told about the twins, my vision, the entrance hall, and how she came to carry Little Fox's bow and arrow.

I led us to the staircase, but halted several feet from the landing. We heard someone coming up. The footsteps were slow and methodical: step, pause, step, pause. We warily approached the top of the stairs and saw a tall shape ascending.

"Is it Mr. Tremblin?" Millie asked.

Demarius was ready to bolt. "Is it Daemon Hall *in* Mr. Tremblin?"

When he got midway up, I called to him. He stopped, gazing blankly ahead, arms hanging at his sides. His clothes were torn, his face was bruised, and old blood crusted under his nose and around his mouth. He slowly lifted his head until he took us in his gaze.

"I don't think he's—" Demarius started to say.

"Get ready to run," I whispered.

Ian Tremblin flung his arms wide and shouted, "Afghanistan banana stand!"

Grinning, he ran up and we rushed down, Demarius helping Matt. We collided on the staircase, which nearly caused us to tumble down. We crowded him with a united hug.

"Oh, thank God, you're safe. Thank God."

We explained why we had to hurry, and also why we were covered in goop.

"Hmmm, ectoplasm is my guess." Ian Tremblin told us that

when Millie had read Lucinda's story, he felt a presence beside him, and the next thing he knew, he was wandering around in the basement. He realized that Daemon Hall had once again slipped into him, and a fight started for possession of his body and soul. He described how the battle with Daemon Hall raged until he literally pummeled himself with punches and blows.

"I didn't think I could win." His voice was tremulous.

"How did you beat it?" Demarius asked.

"I'm not sure it was me. You see, everything began to shake, like an earthquake."

"When Oaskaguakw came through the floor," Millie said.

"Minutes later, Daemon Hall left me."

"I bet that was the exact moment the arrow pierced the book," I said.

Demarius scrutinized his face. "You sure kicked your own ass, Mr. Tremblin."

"That I did, Demarius." He reached up and gingerly touched his chin. "That I did."

We started down the stairs for the second floor, and I actually felt hopeful that we'd all leave in one piece.

Lucinda motioned Millie and me over and took us into her confidence. "I'm worried about Scungilli. He's in a bad way, and I'm not talking about his ankle. I don't remember what happened in Daemon's study. Matt does. He says Rudolph Daemon spoke to him."

"Daemon got hanged before the door closed," I said.

Lucinda nodded. "He died, *then* spoke to Matt. That's why he's freaked."

"What'd Daemon say?"

"He won't talk about it."

Millie sniffed a couple of times, then Lucinda. We smelled smoke.

"It's too late," Matt said, his voice flat.

"No way. Demarius and I made it through this fire already."

"Damn right," Demarius said from beside him. "And we can do it again."

We rushed down to the second-floor landing, where my bravado deflated like a burst balloon. Orange, red, and yellow hues glowed within a rolling sea of smoke so thick that the entrance hall was no longer visible. The crackling sound of fire echoed as the heavy smoke crept up the staircase like rapidly rising fog.

"The floor's hot." I could feel it, even through my shoes. "We'll never get to the front door."

"We're going to die," Matt wailed.

"Back!" Ian Tremblin pointed deeper into the house. "That way!"

They started down the hallway, but I stayed. Something nagged at me.

"Wade, now!" the writer ordered.

"Wait." I looked down at the book in my hands. I had a feeling, an intuition, that I needed to piece together. "All this started when we told stories around this." Coughing, I held up the book.

Millie dropped the bow, ran to me, and tried pulling me along. "Wade, the smoke."

"It traveled with us from Mr. Tremblin's house to here."

Ian Tremblin shouted, "Wade, I don't see—"

I cut him off. "You're the one who said that books transport readers."

"Books do what?" he said, then fell into a fit of coughs.

"The tree and the monsters disappeared when Millie shot the book. Why? She hurt it, wounded it."

"Wade, come on!"

"This is what's been consistent from the start! The book has been making all this happen, like some sort of evil battery powering it all!"

Ian Tremblin stepped toward me, his eyes glued to the *Book of Daemon Hall*. "A potent talisman?"

I held it over my head like a hellfire preacher with a Bible. "Back in his library you said that books and stories take readers to other places and times. It's usually in their heads, but the *Book of Daemon Hall* did it for real."

The writer put a hand on my shoulder and nodded. "I never thought I'd encourage a book burning, but do it, Wade."

Flames danced through the smoke. The heat was intense. Ignoring the yellow smoke engulfing my feet, I hurried to the top step and hurled the book toward the inferno. As the book fell, the paper airplane I'd made from one of its pages slid out, caught an updraft from the fire, and flew out over the entrance hall.

"Now we can go!"

The roar of the firestorm was earsplitting as we ran down the second-floor hallway. Breathing smoke was painful, and it felt like we were running on a stovetop. Ian Tremblin led us, Demarius and Lucinda rushed Matt along, and I pushed from the rear. Everyone vanished in a firestorm as the floor collapsed. We fell screaming into the inferno below—

—and crashed onto the floor back in the library at Tremblin's Lair. We sat up, gazing dumbly at one another as smoke rose from our clothes.

Demarius beat at sparks in his dreadlocks and laughed. "We—we made it."

"We all got out. Even me," Matt said, disbelieving.

Smiling, Lucinda climbed into a chair, several inches of hair singed away.

Millie and I stood and hugged. "No one died." I turned to Ian Tremblin. "No one."

He sat up, grinning like crazy, and balled his hand into a fist. "We beat Daemon Hall, Wade. We beat it."

Epilogue

It's cold enough that we see our breath as we stand next to each other, gloved hand in gloved hand. Millie reaches up to touch the place where her necklace rests under her jacket and shirt. I do the same. We didn't plan it, but for Christmas I gave her a necklace, a red stone mounted in silver. She gave me a blue stone necklace. It seemed proof that we should be together.

Millie was a big help when it came to my parents. I didn't tell them about the *Book of Daemon Hall*. This was kind of risky, as my mom is expert at detecting secrets. But when I told her I'd met someone, she totally focused on that. She and Millie get along great. Millie really clinched it when she called my mom on Christmas Eve and asked if she could go to Christmas mass with my family.

"How are you feeling?" I ask.

"I'm fine. It's only a cold." When I picked her up, she had told me she might be coming down with something. I'd offered to postpone our date to another night, but she insisted on coming. "In fact, I'd lay a big ol' liplock on you, but I don't want to give you my germs."

I turn her so that she folds into my arms, and kiss her.

She leans her head against my shoulder. "If you get sick, don't blame me."

"Typhoid Millie. Now, there's a pen name for you. Speaking of which, did you decide what you'll write about?"

Ian Tremblin had announced that he'd hold no more contests and proclaimed everyone a winner. Millie, Matt, and Lucinda would each pen a novella, longer than a short story and shorter than a novel. Tremblin would edit them, and they would be published in a book as part of his Macabre Master series, just like mine.

"I think I'll write more about Little Fox's adventures." We're quiet awhile, and then she says, "Lucinda called a couple of days ago."

"How's she doing?"

"She's strong, you know—says she's fine. Oh, and Matt had called her. He and Ian Tremblin are e-mailing and IMing each other. They're still debating whether we went back in time or whether Daemon Hall was showing its memories."

I laughed, picturing both of them furiously typing their arguments.

"Who do you think is right?"

"Both . . . neither. It's something we can't explain."

We turn our attention to the mansion on the other side of the fence. It's not a full moon, but big enough that we can see Daemon Hall pretty well. "Millie, I sort of understand why you wanted to come here, but why at night?"

"I want to see it at its scariest. I need to face it so I can face my fear. Maybe it'll end my nightmares."

I've had nightmares, too, but I don't mention the voice that comes when I sleep, saying things I can't quite remember.

"What's that?" Millie's looking toward the mansion.

"Where?"

"Over there, see?" She points up to one of the third-floor windows, to something in the air. "Is it a bird?"

We watch it approach, soaring to the right, gliding to the left. When it gets close enough to recognize, my heart feels like it's squeezed in a vise. I hear an intake of breath from Millie as she, too, identifies it. Neither of us speaks as the paper airplane I made from a page of the *Book of Daemon Hall* sails closer, finally landing at our feet.

With a shaking hand, I reach for the plane. Millie grabs my arm, and I pause to look at her; her face is white and her eyes wide. She shakes her head, but I pick it up anyway. Just touching the paper makes my stomach roll. We get back into my brother's VW. I start the engine and mess with the heater, then turn on the dome light.

Millie touches my arm. "How?"

I shrug. When it comes to Daemon Hall, I've stopped asking questions.

"Should we unfold it?"

"Yeah, I guess so." Opening it carefully, I hold it against the dashboard. At the top is the same pen-and-ink drawing of the skull and crossed pens that headed the table of contents in the *Book of Daemon Hall*. "Remember when I pulled the arrow out of the book and this page came out?"

She nodded. "We never looked at it, did we?"

"I thought it was another blank page." It isn't. Little boxes and rectangles are drawn all over it. "What do you think it means?"

Millie shakes her head.

I look closer and see tiny squiggles.

"Hang on." I get out, open the trunk, and start rooting around the assortment of junk my brother has stuffed in there over the years, looking for an old magnifying glass I'd come across a couple of months earlier. I find it, return to the driver's seat, and hold the glass over the paper.

"Is that writing?" she asks.

"Yeah." In each square are handwritten words. I squint hard. "I think it's a map of Daemon Hall. See, in that first big rectangle it says 'Entrance Hall.' And, look, there's the dining room, first-floor library, and so on."

"Wait a minute, Wade." She points about halfway down the front page. "Daemon Hall is only so big, right? But the rooms continue all the way to the bottom of the map. It's not that big."

"Weird." I look closely, then flip the map over and see there are hundreds, maybe thousands, more rooms, halls, wings, and annexes that don't exist. "Daemon Hall would have to be as big as a whole town or city for all of that."

I hunch over the magnifying glass and look at several non-existent rooms. "This just gets stranger."

"What?"

"Instead of saying what the rooms are, they have names, dates, and times printed next to them. Here's one room: The name written there is Oliver Snelling. It also says June 2, 1952, and 3:13 A.M."

"Could that be someone who was lost or killed in Daemon Hall on that date and at that time?"

"Maybe." I scan some more of the squares. "Wait, no, because the dates don't all fit. Check this one out, Emily Packard, September 18, 1798, 10:11 P.M. That's over a hundred years before Daemon Hall was built."

Millie takes the magnifying glass and holds it over the middle of the parchment. "Is that a tower?"

"Looks like the kind of thing Rapunzel was imprisoned in, huh? But why draw the actual tower?" All the other rooms are drawn as squares, like they're being viewed from above, but the tower is complete as if seen from the side.

Millie takes the magnifier and leans close. "Gross."

"What?"

She points at the top of the tower and hands me the magnifying glass. "It's a heart."

Not the Valentine's Day variety, but the kind that looks freshly ripped from someone's chest. I point to more writing and whisper, "The heart of Daemon Hall."

"Can we—should we try and figure out what the map is for?"

"I don't know. Part of me wants to. The other part says we should leave it alone, that it'll only lead to trouble."

Millie looks at me. "All those names, those people, what if they're imprisoned by Daemon Hall, or their souls are, like your friend Chelsea was?"

"What can we do? We nearly died in there."

She nods, then coughs.

"Maybe I should send it to Mr. Tremblin. He's good at figuring out stuff like this. What do you think?"

Millie doesn't answer, instead she grasps my arm. Her face is pale, almost white. She swallows repeatedly.

"Are you all right?"

She shakes her head. "All of a sudden I feel awful."

"I'll take you home."

Her face is flushed pink. I touch her cheek and she's burning with fever. I turn off the dome light and reach for the keys dangling in the ignition as my cell phone rings. I answer, intending to tell whoever it is I'll call back later.

"Hey, I'll have to get back—"

"It wasn't ectoplasm," someone shouts.

"What?"

"We made a mistake!"

I recognize the voice. "Matt?"

"We're in big trouble. You didn't figure it out," he says accusingly, then admits, "I missed it too."

"Slow down and tell me what's wrong." I look at Millie. She has her head back and eyes closed. She's shivering.

"Ian Tremblin is in a coma!"

"What?"

"We were instant messaging, arguing our Daemon Hall time theories, and he just stopped. I called and Mrs. Rathbone told me."

"Told you what?"

"I tried getting in touch with Lucinda to tell her."

"You're not making sense."

"Her parents told me she's in the hospital."

"Hospital?"

"She's real sick, high fever, and they don't know what it is."

A chill starts at the top of my head and runs in waves down my body.

"Demarius?"

"His mom said he can't come to the phone because he's sick

in bed!" Matt is close to tears. "And I'm not feeling so good myself."

"The tree—the ectoplasm," I mutter.

"We're screwed. It was the same stuff that sprayed the construction workers when they cut down the tree, the ones who
got sick and slipped into comas. Remember them? Their spines
snapped, and they died. That's going to be us! It got on you and
Millie, and then we found you guys and everybody hugged,
spreading it all around."

I want to shout at Matt, tell him he's wrong.

He starts crying. "Want to know what Rudolph Daemon
said to me in his study? Remember that? I wouldn't tell anyone."

"What did—" The question catches in my throat.

"Lucinda and I couldn't do anything when Daemon was
hanged. We watched until he quit kicking. Then something
happened—Lucinda froze, stood there without moving. I
screamed at her, but she wouldn't snap out of it. I looked up. Even
though he was dead, Rudolph Daemon, noose around his neck,
looked down. I could tell he felt sorry for me. That's funny, isn't
it? He's hanging by the neck, and he feels sorry for me. Then he
said, 'You'll return, Matthew. Even if you're dead.'"

The phone slips from my hand. "Millie?" She's panting hard.
I shake her shoulder and shout, "Millie!"

I start the car. Twisting the wheel, I speed up the dirt road.
My head pounds, and my back aches. In fact, I ache all over. I

put the back of my hand to my forehead. Too hot. We need to get to the hospital fast.

I glance in the rearview mirror as we race from Daemon Hall. There are red lights in two of the third-floor windows. In between them and a floor down, a single window glows red. The same shade of light flares through the double-door entrance. Daemon Hall, at that moment, resembles a skull.

And now I remember what that voice says, the one that comes in my nightmares. Like Rudolph Daemon said to Matt, the voice in my dreams says, "You'll return to Daemon Hall. Alive or dead, you'll be back."